Liam and Cecelia

" Ye have bewitched me, Cecelia."

Christmas in the Scot's Arms

Highlander Vows: Entangled Hearts,
Book Three

by
Julie Johnstone

The best way to stay in touch is to subscribe to my newsletter. Go to www.juliejohnstoneauthor.com and subscribe in the box at the top of the page that says Newsletter. If you don't hear from me once a month, please check your spam filter and set up your email to allow my messages through to you so you don't miss the opportunity to win great prizes or hear about appearances.

Dedication

This book is for everyone who needs to feel the hope of love at Christmastime.

Special thanks go out to my husband, who truly went above and beyond to give me the time needed to write this book, and to my children, who tiptoed around me as I wrote.

If you're interested in when my books go on sale, or want to be one of the first to know about my new releases, please follow me on BookBub! You'll get quick book notifications every time there's a new pre-order, book on sale, or new release with an easy click of your mouse to follow me. You can follow me on BookBub here:
www.bookbub.com/authors/julie-johnstone

One

London, England
1815

Lying was a sin. Yet sometimes, one was given no choice but to lie. For example, if one was trying to protect one's dearly departed father's good name, sometimes one must lie. Or if one had a mother who was being positively unreasonable, sometimes one must lie. Even though Miss Cecelia Cartwright was sure she had legitimate reasons for what she was doing, guilt plagued her. Hence her new habit of reminding God exactly why he should forgive her for her trespasses.

Cecelia dashed a look behind her as she tiptoed past her mother's bedchamber, down the stairs, and toward the front door of their townhome. She gripped her most prized possession in one hand—a book of poetry by Lord Byron that her father had given her—and her shoes in the other. Every astute schemer knew that shoes made entirely too much noise on hardwood floors, and since her mother had deemed Lady Elizabeth Burton unacceptable for Cecelia to associate with and had forbidden her from visiting Elizabeth, Cecelia had been forced to become an expert conniver.

Her mother had always been a worrisome sort, particularly about what others might think of them, but compassion had tempered her concerns, and she had never snubbed someone purposely simply because the *ton* had done so. But two years ago, when money had first started to seem scarce and her mother had discovered Cecelia's father had been gambling, a bit of Mother's compassion had disappeared. Instead, it was replaced by a need to make sure they did everything they could to maintain their place in Society. Then last year, when Father had gambled away almost all their money—and his life right along with it—every iota of empathy her mother had possessed had disappeared. Cecelia understood, of course. Her mother had come from poverty, and after she'd married Father, who'd had money at the time, Mother had never felt as though she was quite good enough. It made her fiercely determined never to return to a state of want nor let Cecelia be thrust into that same fate.

These familiar thoughts tumbled through Cecelia's head as she crept along, diverting her attention from where she was stepping. The moment the splintered wood caught on the right toe of her last pair of good stockings, she cursed her carelessness and shook her head. She wiggled her foot, trying to free herself, but her efforts were for naught. The sliver of wood had gone through her stockings and pierced her skin.

Blast. She'd get a lecture for that, and rightly so. They had no spare coin to purchase such luxuries as stockings. The meager funds that had been left after her father had died were rapidly dwindling. She'd done what she could, such as taking on the task of shopping herself. She actually quite enjoyed going down to the market and bargaining with the vendors. She'd convinced her mother to teach her how to cook, as well, and that had allowed Mother to let go of their cook.

She knew Mother would have helped more, but her hands ached so much some days that she could hardly use them. Cecelia had also convinced her mother to teach her to wash and clean, so they no longer needed a maid. Mother had protested, of course, reminding Cecelia that she was sure the problem with her hands was from years of such labor, but when Cecelia had shown her the money they would save, Mother had relented. The only servant they still had was the butler, and that was only because Mother had said they must retain him to keep up appearances in case they had a caller. But no one ever called, not since Cecelia had been labeled *disgraced*.

Cecelia shook off the depressing thought and continued toward the front door. Tiny slivers of sunlight shone in through the cracks of the overly weathered door. Dismay filled her. It wasn't simply the door. Being upset over a door would be silly; however, the sorry state of the door represented the sorry state of their affairs. So much needed repairing, but there was no money with which to repair it. Tonight, she promised herself, she would once again try to convince Mother to allow her to search for seamstress work.

Cecelia cringed thinking about how that conversation had gone last time. It had started with her mother screeching that if Cecelia did that, their only real hope—which Mother firmly believed was for Cecelia to somehow return to the *ton's* good graces and marry well—would be lost, and poverty would claim them. The conversation had ended in blessed silence, but only because poor Mother had fainted. From all her screeching, no doubt.

Lifting up on the door handle to ease its squeak, Cecelia held her breath. Thankfully, the door released without a sound, and she could safely exhale. She pulled the door open.

"Oh!" she gasped, as a gust of wintery wind hit her in the face. Frowning, she eyed the sky accusingly. How could the sun be shining yet it be so cold outside? As if in answer, a larger, particularly ominous-looking cloud moved in front of the sun. She laughed in spite of the shiver another burst of wind had caused in her.

"I suppose that is your way of answering me, God," she said under her breath while gently easing the door shut.

She tucked her book under her arm and bent down to put on her shoes. She could not stay at Elizabeth's for more than one hour. Mother's afternoon nap never lasted longer than that, and as market day was tomorrow, Cecelia could not use the chore as an excuse for where she had gone. Her mother had a suspicious mind—for good reason, Cecelia supposed—but that did not change the fact that she would likely take to following Cecelia if she thought her daughter was doing something that would endanger her return to Society. And Cecelia needed her friendship with Elizabeth. It kept her sane.

Shoving her quickly freezing feet into her slippers, she jerked upright, grasped her book, and started down the short, stone staircase without gripping the iron railing. The moment her right foot landed on the second step and the slick ice whipped her forward, she realized her mistake. She flailed her arms in a desperate attempt to regain her balance, but instead, she managed to lose it altogether. Her left foot joined her right in sliding out from under her, and before she could even release a scream, her feet—and her book—flew into the air. She landed hard upon her back, half on the bottom step and half on the walkway.

A burst of air released from her lungs, along with a groan as small dots of black with specks of brightness danced in her vision. She squeezed her eyes shut against the instant ache in her head, and the thud of rushing footsteps told her she had a witness to her clumsiness and humiliation. Forcing herself to open her eyes, she pressed her palms against the icy ground and dug her heels in to try to gain purchase, but the result was her body sliding all the way off the bottom step and onto the walkway.

Sitting up, she turned her head to see who was approaching, but the corner of her prized book floating in a puddle caught her attention. It was the last gift her father had ever given her, and she let out a strangled cry as she attempted to move from her bottom to her knees. Slipping and sliding on the ice, she managed to reach the book. She went to pluck it from the water, and it caught on a fallen branch, ripping out several pages of the soggy book.

"Oh dear!" she exclaimed on a choked sob.

"Are ye injured, lass?" inquired a concerned male voice with the deepest timbre and smoothest Scottish brogue she'd ever heard.

With her palms stinging from the ice, her knees throbbing against the unforgiving surface, and her heart broken over her ruined book, she could do little more than glance upward, her vision blurry with sudden unshed tears, and say in a strained voice, "My book is ruined. I—" She sniffled and blinked the mortifying tears from her eyes. She simply had to get control of herself!

"Please forgive me," she said. "It was the last present my father gave me before he passed."

With one more good blink, her vision cleared, and her mouth gaped open in shock. The most exquisitely handsome man was towering over her. He had a strong jaw and perfectly carved features. Before she could really scrutinize him, he kneeled, bringing his face a hairsbreadth from hers.

Worried green eyes locked on her, and a tingle started in her stomach that seemed to move to all her limbs. She'd never seen such bright eyes in her life. Jonathan Hunt—she clenched her teeth at the thought of the man to whom she'd been betrothed, and whom was now betrothed to her former best friend, Matilda—had dark eyes, which should have been a sign. Dark eyes for a dark heart.

The Scot glanced toward her book. "Don't be sorry for yer sadness over such a treasure being destroyed. I lost a cuff that my father had given me in a fall from a tower, and the grief is still with me. It was the last thing my father had gifted me, as well, so I understand."

Cecelia was so touched by his words, honesty, and kindness that tears welled in her eyes once again. "Thank you," she whispered.

"It is customary to help up a fallen woman, Liam, not make her cry!" an agitated feminine voice interrupted. She, too, had a strong Scottish brogue.

Cecelia slowly turned her now-pounding head in the direction of the new voice, her cheeks burning with embarrassment. This was simply awful! She'd been so busy gawking that she'd not even noticed the woman's approach, and Cecelia was still sprawled on the ground!

Before she could rectify her unladylike position, the handsome Scot held out his hands to her. She blinked, uncertain whether to take his aid or attempt, yet again, to stand on her own, but when he said, "I can pick ye up, if ye wish it," she quickly shook her head.

"That won't be necessary, Mr....?"

"Liam," he replied, grabbing her hands and hauling her up with such swift efficiency that her head spun. As her body shifted dangerously forward, she placed a steadying hand out, which to her horror, landed on his broad, extremely solid chest. This man was certainly no soft fop.

She snatched her hand back but noticed the corners of his mouth tilt up into a smile. "I beg your pardon," she offered, forcing herself not to mumble the apology in her discomfiture. If she'd learned one thing this year while weathering snubs from the *ton*, pretending not to hear snickers behind the fans of ladies she had once called friends, and hiding the true state of her family's financial affairs daily, it was that appearing unaffected was the best shield against the pain. She rather thought she had become quite adept at it. Well, until her gawking of moments ago.

"It's Liam who should be begging yer pardon at grabbing ye and hauling ye up like a brute," said the petite, red-haired woman who smiled so genuinely at Cecelia that she found her defenses lowering as she smiled back. Oh, but it had been a long time since she'd passed someone on the street in this neighborhood and not felt judged. Her heart squeezed.

"Aila," Liam said, speaking directly to the redheaded woman in a warning tone.

The woman, Aila, responded with a chuckle as she cocked her head and stared at Cecelia. Aila had the same mesmerizingly green eyes as Liam. In fact, their eyes were so similar that the two had to be related.

"I'm Aila MacLeod," the woman said. She waved a hand at the man. "And this is my brother Liam. We are guests of the Duke and Duchess of Rochburn. Do ye know them?"

"Yes," Cecelia said warily, anything but thrilled at the memories the mere mention of the Rochburn name stirred, since it was in their home that her reputation had been destroyed. On the other hand, she was glad there would be no more talk of her embarrassing tumble.

"It's a pleasure to meet you both," she hurried on, refusing to acknowledge how they had met. "I'm Miss Cartwright," she added, gripping her ruined book tightly.

"Well, Miss Cartwright, who reads…" He glanced down at the spine of her book, and his eyes widened. "Ye read Byron?" he asked with obvious surprise.

She could not help the smirk that pulled at her lips. "You speak of Byron as if you know his work," she replied, giving him the same sort of insult he'd just given her.

He chuckled. "I deserved that. I'm sorry. Most of the ladies I've met in England have seemed—"

"Unintelligent?" Cecelia supplied for him with a grin. "More concerned with fashion than literature?"

"Aye," he relented with an apologetic look.

"Well, Mr. MacLeod—"

"It's Lord MacLeod," his sister interjected. "But just barely."

Cecelia frowned. Did the woman mean he was poor? She must, but why was she smirking at her brother then? Poverty hardly seemed like something to be smirking about.

"Ye were saying, Miss Cartwright," Liam asked.

"Oh!" She felt her neck grow hot. "I'm not like most women of the *ton*."

"If that's true," he replied, his tone teasing, "then ye will tell me yer Christian name. I find it humorous that all the ladies here seem so shocked when I ask for it." His shining green eyes swept from her feet to her face, making her awfully glad she had donned her emerald-and-white day gown, which still looked lovely despite being made two Seasons ago. When his gaze met hers, there was no mistaking the challenge shining in their depths.

Her mouth gaped open. Liam's sister gasped as she poked her brother in the arm. He did not so much as flick his attention to his sister but kept it squarely on Cecelia, his eyebrows arching high, as if daring her to break the dictates of decorum. She'd been a rule breaker previously, which was why everyone in the *ton* had been so quick to believe the worst about her. In fact, the beginning of her downfall had all started with an ill-advised horse race in Hyde Park with the Duke of Blackmore and had progressed from that incident to an imprudent frolic in the Serpentine with her shoes and stockings off. Once again, with Blackmore.

Or perhaps the true start of it all had been years before due to her inability to follow the rules of etiquette that Society demanded. She found them ridiculous, despite her mother's constant reminders that the rules determined the difference between the upper and lower classes. However her downfall had started, once kindled, it had forced her to accept Jonathan Hunt's—or Viscount Hawkins's—marriage offer when he'd made it because, by then, Mother had learned of Father's gambling problem and both her parents had feared she might not get another offer since the whispers in the *ton* of her hoydenish propensities had grown deafening. Jonathan had not seemed to believe the whispers, which she had thought said something good about his character. She should have known better.

That "good character" had disappeared about as fast as it had taken her to spit out the embarrassing sentence that she no longer had a dowry. She was fairly certain she'd not even inhaled a breath after completing the sentence before Jonathan had demanded the betrothal be broken.

"Let me handle how to announce it," Jonathan had said. More the fool was she for having gone along with that plea. He'd handled it, all right. Somehow, he'd convinced Lord Tarrymount—his crony in crime—to lure her into the library at the Rochburns' home and then kiss her just as a group of the *ton's* biggest gossips strolled in—with Jonathan among them, of course. He had somehow managed to look like the injured party, and she looked like a woman of easy virtue.

He'd also promised that he'd keep the secret of her father's near-penniless state. Technically, the blackguard *had* kept that secret, but the price of his silence was her good name, and after she had confronted him about what he and Lord Tarrymount had done to her, the price of Jonathan's silence was her own silence. If she dared cry foul, he'd let her family's financial situation be known. She'd been unwise, albeit unwittingly, but that had not changed a thing.

Since her disgrace had occurred, she'd broken nary a rule, not that she'd had much chance since the *ton's* doors had been firmly shut in her face. Yet, even if the chance had arisen, she would not have dared to take it. She knew how much her mother hoped all would be forgotten in time and that Cecelia might still make a good match.

"Please do ignore Liam," Aila said, disrupting Cecelia's terrible recollections, thank heavens. Cecelia focused her attention on Aila just as she gave her brother a disgruntled look. "He does not care for the rules of English Society. He does not understand the necessity."

Cecelia felt her frown deepen as she dragged her gaze back to the compelling Scot. Frankly, she had never understood the need for all the rules, either, which was why she had not bothered overly much to heed them. She still didn't comprehend what was so god-awful about sharing your Christian name, but with all her troubles, she really should just abide by the rules that had been hammered into her since birth.

She narrowed her eyes as she watched Liam's eyebrow arch ever higher. Challenging. Mocking.

Botheration! She'd never been one to pass up a challenge. She darted a look up and down the street to ensure that they were alone. "Cecelia," she announced triumphantly.

"That's a lovely name, lass," he replied in a deep, sensual tone that made her skin prickle.

The compliment this virtual stranger had just offered pleased her so much that she wanted to grin, but somehow, she managed to make her mouth behave and appear unaffected, which was quite properly English. She had already broken one rule of etiquette today; she dared not break another so quickly. It was like tempting fate to slap her.

"Thank you," she replied, trying desperately not to sound breathy with her happiness.

Liam's mouth tugged farther upward at the corners, and she suspected she had failed miserably at hiding her pleasure in his compliment, but before he could say anything else, his sister spoke. "Have ye been to the Rochburns' home before?"

"Yes, but not in quite some time. You see, I don't get about much socially," Cecelia said, praying her tone did not sound strained as she glanced toward the townhome of which they spoke. Her happiness abruptly vanished. Cecelia's family had once been welcomed at the Rochburns', but after her disgrace, that had changed. *Everything* had changed. And a sennight later, her father had drunk himself to death.

When Aila loudly cleared her throat, Cecelia flinched, realizing she was expected to elaborate. She had no notion of what to say. Heat burned her cheeks so greatly that she pressed her hands to them. "I'm terribly sorry," she mumbled, searching for a passable excuse. "The cold makes me, um..."

"Freezes yer tongue, aye? It does that to mine." Liam gave her a look of encouragement, and she knew the man had purposely just offered her a perfect excuse for her rudeness. She liked this man more than she liked most any lord she'd met in her past two Seasons on the marriage mart, despite knowing him for less than an hour.

She found herself nodding.

A slow smile spread across his face and made her heart tug. He was breathtakingly, ruggedly manly. He reminded her of the naked Greek statues she'd seen at the museum with her father. Except, of course, this man was clothed. She gulped just thinking about the scandalous prospect of his nudity, and when she brought her gaze to his once more, she found him staring intently, as if he knew her secret thoughts. Embarrassed, she focused on his sister, but she could feel his eyes upon her just as sure as she could feel the heat of the sun.

Aila turned and glanced down the street toward the Rochburns' townhome. "'Tis funny, I thought I'd met all the family's neighbors…"

Cecelia shifted from foot to foot, the uncomfortable knowledge of why the Rochburns had not mentioned her knotting her stomach. "Are you, er, particular friends of Her Grace's?" Cecelia stumbled, finding it hard to believe the stuffy Duchess of Rochburn would befriend poor Scots, let alone have them as guests in her home.

Aila chuckled, and her brother frowned. "I am to marry her son," she said.

Cecelia blinked in surprise. "Lord Aldridge?" Sadness tugged at her. They had once been good friends, but that was likely never to be again. "I hadn't realized he'd returned from the fight against Napoleon." Richard Stone, Marquess of Aldridge was the Duke of Rochburn's only heir, and the man, to his credit, had defied his father and gone off to fight Napoleon.

"He has only just returned." Aila surprised Cecelia by grabbing her hand. "Oh! We are having a grand ball to celebrate our betrothal! Ye must come! Ye are the first woman my age here I have met who I think I might actually like! It would be lovely to have a friend—"

"No!" Cecelia snapped, not meaning to be rude, but she certainly could not let this woman, who seemed so nice, return to the Duke and Duchess of Rochburn's home and voice her wish to invite Cecelia to the ball. They'd laugh Aila out of their presence and may even doubt her worthiness for Aldridge.

When Cecelia realized Aila was gawking at her and Liam had a puzzled look on his face, she scrambled to come up with an explanation. "I, um, I detest balls." Heat from the lie singed her cheeks, her neck, and her chest. "I really must go." She offered a quick curtsy, but as she started to step around Liam, Aila touched her arm.

"I detest balls, too, but I would so dearly love to see ye there. I will have Richard invite ye, and ye may decline or accept as ye wish."

The thought of going back to the Rochburns' made her ill, but as she was positive the opportunity would not truly arise, she nodded.

A sudden thought struck her. What if she really could somehow manage to get back into the good graces of the *ton*? She would do it for her mother's sake. Or she would at least try.

Even as she now prayed that she would receive an invitation, she pleaded to God that Jonathan not be there. Her palms still itched to slap him when she thought about what he had done to her, and her heart squeezed when she thought upon Matilda.

"Thank you," she murmured, hoping it sounded genuine. She thought she might have succeeded, given Aila's grin, but when Cecelia stole a glance at Liam, his narrowed, questioning eyes were trained on her.

Two

Liam had come to this godforsaken place for two reasons. One was to ensure his younger sister was marrying a good man. His father had been dying when he had given Aila his approval to marry Aldridge, and with Father's clouded mind and the clan's unstable finances at the time, Liam feared his father might not have made a well-thought-out decision. And since Liam had been off fighting Napoleon when Aila had actually met Aldridge, Liam wanted to meet the marquess and judge for himself if the man was worthy of his sister.

The other reason he was in London was to avoid, if only for a little while, the plethora of lasses wishing to marry him now that he was laird of the MacLeod clan. He would be flattered, except he was not a fool. He understood that a great deal of his appeal was derived from the fact that he was now the leader of one of the few remaining stable and wealthy clans in the Highlands. The Jacobite rising had spawned a cleansing of those who had not supported King George II, and it had forever diminished the very way of life of the clans. The constant peril and turmoil that followed made stability and prosperity rare to find. But before his father had passed, he had sold some land, and in doing so, the clan's future had become financially secure once again.

He was now considered a prize to be won by the lasses,

their mother's, and most especially, the lairds of the other clans looking to make an alliance with the MacLeods by way of marriage. Liam did not much care for feeling like a fat pig, and he had long wished to marry a woman who held his heart, as was tradition in his family. He preferred to be judged and desired for who he was, without the trappings of money. Yet that seemed more and more of an impossibility in Scotland where everyone knew of him.

Perchance it was an impossibility everywhere, though. He had half hoped that coming to England would give him an opportunity to meet ladies who knew nothing of his clan, but it seemed the MacLeod reputation had preceded him.

Aila loudly cleared her throat and jerked him back to the moment. "Liam will walk ye where ye are going. I'd hate for ye to slip again."

He was on the verge of offering an excuse as to why he could not, as it had become his custom to avoid being lured into any situation where a lass could claim he had compromised her and then demand he marry her for honor's sake, but he swallowed his pretext. Cecelia—for he refused to think of her as Miss Cartwright—had piqued his curiosity. Any lady who read Byron, teared up at a destroyed book from her father, and shared his opinion that most ladies of the *ton* were dim, was a lady with whom he wanted to become better acquainted. Not to mention she clearly did not know who he was, and he liked that very much.

Beyond being intriguing, she was also the most breathtaking woman he had ever beheld. Her gleaming, long, black hair and her tawny eyes framed by thick lashes stirred his desire *and* further ignited his curiosity. She had a certain wariness in her gaze, yet pride in her stance, and he found he wanted to know what caused both.

He proffered his elbow. "I'd be happy to escort ye, *Miss Cartwright.*" He could not help but instill a teasing note in his voice as he said her name and was surprised at himself for doing so. It was not like him to flirt with the lasses, and his sister's wide eyes told him she had recognized what he was doing, too. He schooled his features, not wishing to encourage Aila to try pairing him with Cecelia. It would be just like his meddling sister to attempt such a thing.

Cecelia bit her lip adorably, showing her hesitancy. He realized with a start that he was facing a most novel and most prized situation. Here was a lady who had no notion of who he was, so if she chose to take his arm, she would be doing so based solely on her interest and possible attraction to him. His pulse quickened at the chance before him.

For a long moment, she stood silent, indecision playing across her face. Not a great thing for his pride, yet it oddly pleased him that she had not rushed to take the opportunity to walk with him.

"All right," she relented, sounding as if she was agreeing to be escorted to the guillotine. He should have been offended, but instead he was amused and further enthralled.

He caught Aila's smile and knew she had heard the reluctance, too. Her next words confirmed it. "Ye're good for Liam. He's used to the lasses being more than willing to walk anywhere with him, not that he ever actually allows them to do so." His sister gave him a look that said she was worried for him, which he had grown quite adept at ignoring.

"Oh!" Bright pink infused Cecelia's cheeks. "I'm sure you are used to hordes of eager girls." Her gaze raked over him from head to foot, and then her eyes widened as they met his once more before she jerked her attention back to Aila.

Cecelia displayed a refreshing inability—or unwillingness—to lie. Either way, he found himself grinning at her and hoping she'd grace him with bit more of her company. "Shall we?" he asked.

Slowly, she brought her gaze to his, and he noticed a gold rim around each of her eyes.

Fascinating.

She licked her upper lip and then her bottom lip as she slipped her small hand into the crook of his arm. "I really should not allow—You see, it's simply that—" He watched as she bit down hard on her bottom lip, and a deep curiosity filled him regarding what had her so vexed.

"Botheration!" she finally blurted, ruffling a lock of hair that had fallen over the right side of her face. "Never mind." She eyed the ground warily for a moment as she pointed her toe and gently tapped the ice. "It *is* rather icy, isn't it?"

He nodded, fully entertained by the war going on within her. This situation was so foreign and welcome to him. This…this was exactly what he had been hoping to find in London—the thrill of chance, the uncertainty of a courtship where the outcome was not known simply because he had money.

Finally, Cecelia looked up and gave a decisive nod. "You may escort me, but let us hurry."

He felt a strange sense of accomplishment that this woman had given him her trust, if only for a moment. Her suddenly guarded eyes told him she did not give it often, or easily.

He glanced at his sister. "Will ye be all right to make yer way to the Rochburns' home?" he asked, even though Aila tromping around on an icy walkway didn't worry him in the least. They came from rugged, wild land, and this small bit of ice should hardly give her pause. Still, he doubted

Cecelia understood that, and he did not want to seem uncaring.

"Aye." Aila nodded. "I'll see ye shortly." She gave him a stern look as her eyes darted between him and Cecelia. He blinked in amusement that his sister seemed to feel an odd protectiveness over this woman they had just met. While he had the same stirrings, what did Aila think of him? That he was a rutting beast who would steal a kiss from a lady or take advantage? He glared and was pleased when Aila looked properly reprimanded and apologetic.

As his sister walked away, he turned toward Cecelia and was once more struck by her loveliness. "Where am I to walk ye?"

"To the end of the street to see my friend Lady Burton."

He glanced in the direction she pointed. "The home with the red door?"

She nodded, and a shaft of disappointment shot through him. That was not a long walk. It would not be near enough time to learn much about Cecelia. With this in mind, he made the decision to discard a good deal of small talk and inquire about what he really wanted to know.

"Why do ye not wish to come to the Rochburns' ball?" he asked.

Her bow-shaped lips parted with surprise. "Are you always so blunt, Lord Mac—"

"Liam, I told ye, and aye," he said with a nod.

A crease appeared between her dark eyebrows. "It's not proper for me to call you by your Christian name."

"Do ye always do what's proper?" he teased and then paused, shocked by himself. What had overcome him? He had teased this woman twice in a short span of time. But when she colored fiercely and her chest rose with a sharp breath, he found he was glad something strange had taken hold of him.

"Yes," she growled as she quirked her head in thought. "Is it customary in the Highlands to call people by their Christian names?"

"Aye," he answered, stealing a side glance as they walked so he could see her face again. The vehemence her tone had held seconds before surprised him, but she again spoke before he could question her about it.

"If we chance across each other and no one else is around, you may call me Cecelia," she whispered, as if someone might overhear, "and I will call you Liam. But *please*, I beg of you, if you ever see me when someone else is near, you shall call me Miss Cartwright and I shall call you Lord MacLeod. Do we have an agreement?"

He didn't hesitate to nod. He could sense how important this was to her.

This time the emotion that swept across her face—stark relief—made his chest squeeze. She was so worried over something that seemed so harmless to him. He was not even sure why it unsettled him, as he had only just met her.

"Liam, did you hear me?"

Chuckling, he slowed his step a bit, hoping to prolong their time together. "Nay. I was woolgathering. I beg yer pardon."

She waved her hand airily and offered a genuine smile that was more glorious than any cloudless day in the Highlands. "Oh," she said in an understanding voice, "it's quite all right. I woolgather all the time!"

He never did. Ever. He was single-minded, purposeful, and driven in every action and thought. Always. As laird of the MacLeod clan, he had to be, which left him more than confused by how this woman he had just met had managed to make him act out of character. "What did ye ask me?"

Her smile turned thoughtful, causing two dimples to appear on her face. He wanted to run the pad of his finger over the indentations. "I asked what you thought of London," she said. "Or have you been here before?"

He shook his head. "This is the first time, but so far, I must admit I don't care for London."

"I don't care for it, either," she replied, surprising him with her honest remark.

He ceased walking, though that meant they were now standing in front of the home with the red door. Facing her, he said, "Because of the insipid women of the *ton*?"

She laughed, and every single thing about it beckoned to him. Her head tilted to the right, making her hair fall over her petite shoulder and inviting him to touch the silky tresses. Her eyes sparkled, and the sound of her laughter—Ah, but he could listen to that light, musical note all night long.

"Yes," she said once she had gotten her laughter under control. "And the gentlemen who have no right to put the word *gentle* in front of the word *men*."

He didn't know who had wronged her, but he had a sudden burning desire to use his fists. "I'm sorry," he replied, seeing pain flash in her eyes.

She pressed her hands to her cheeks. "I should not have said that!" Her eyes rounded, looking very much like two large walnuts faded to a golden color by the summer sun. "I don't know what came over me to speak so plainly. I daresay, I know better."

"I rather like yer plain speech," he admitted, happily taking his cue from her. "There does not seem to be much of it here in London. Where I live on the Isle of Skye in Scotland, true speech is our way."

When her mouth parted slightly, he wasn't sure if he

had offended her, so he added, "Or perhaps I've simply misjudged?"

"No," she said with a laugh that lacked the bitterness he might have expected given her remarks of moments ago about the gentlemen. "You've not misjudged. One rarely hears the truth from another in the *ton*. The way here is to speak what you know someone wants to hear, unless you truly dislike the person or think he or she is not even worth speaking to at all. Then you either give him or her the cut direct or gossip about him or her in whispers behind your fan."

As she relayed the information, her face displayed one emotion after another, and he found himself unable to look away. Anger, hurt, and defiance flitted across her face, and finally, the acceptance of the inevitable settled on her delicate features. It angered him that she would accept such things, as he felt sure she spoke from personal experience.

"Is this what ye do or others do?" he inquired, seeking to ensure he was not misunderstanding simply because he was attracted to her.

She paused and offered him a startled look. "Me? Oh, no, I would never do such a thing, which I'm sure is one of my gravest flaws."

"I've a hard time imagining ye have any," he replied, hearing the huskiness in his voice.

Her lashes swept downward to veil her eyes for a moment before she met his gaze with her now-serious one. "You've only just met me. I assure you, I have many."

"Name one," he challenged, reveling in the easy, honest banter.

She pressed her lips together on a smirk. "I have spoken far more honestly than is wise. I'm not sure why." She stared at him as if she was trying to untangle a knot and he was the knot.

"Perhaps ye feel comfortable with me because I am a stranger."

A shy look swept across her face, and he decided it was his favorite so far.

"Perhaps," she replied, biting her lip once again. She glanced toward the door. "I better be going. I only have a short time to visit with my friend."

"Do ye have someone waiting on ye?" He sincerely hoped it was not a man.

She nodded. "My mother," she offered with a groan.

He didn't want to part ways with her, yet he could not think of a good reason to tarry. He suddenly found himself looking forward to his sister's betrothal ball if Cecelia was going to be there. But would she come?

"Why do ye not wish to attend the Rochburns' ball?" he asked again, thinking to dissuade her from rejecting the invitation if he could.

Splotches of red touched her cheeks, and he almost wished to take back the question to save her obvious embarrassment. "I have reason to think they would not want me there, but even if they agree to it to please your sister, I doubt I would truly be welcome."

He cocked his head, confused. "Why would ye not be welcome?"

She paused, her chestnut eyes beseeching him. "Please, please do not ask. It's so pleasant to have had a few minutes to talk to someone who does not know me. I know that sounds odd—"

"It doesn't," he interrupted, meaning it. He felt the exact same way.

She gave him a grateful look as she glanced once more toward the door. "I really must go," she said, turning to him. Her loose hair brushed against her cheek, and she reached up and tucked it firmly behind her ear.

"Might I call on ye?" he blurted, deciding to seize the opportunity before him.

Before she could answer, a voice called from behind him, "Ah, Lord MacLeod!"

Liam turned and barely stifled an annoyed groan. "Good afternoon, Tarrymount. Are ye making yer way to see Aldridge?"

Tarrymount nodded. "Do you think we will be able to pry him away from your charming sister to go to White's? I'd love to show you the club."

Liam certainly hoped not. He could not think of anything less enjoyable than spending the evening with Tarrymount, who was a pompous ass.

"Tarrymount, might I present Miss Cartwright," Liam said, turning to make the acquaintances of the two on the chance they did not know each other. But with just one look at Cecelia's colorless face and pinched lips, he knew she was already acquainted with Tarrymount. And not in a positive manner.

"Miss Cartwright," Tarrymount said, looking almost as uncomfortable as Cecelia. "I—It has been quite some time." He gave his cravat a vicious tug.

"Yes," Cecelia replied, her voice a wobbly, pained whisper that drew Liam's gaze immediately to her. "I—" She pressed her hand to her neck, where color had flushed her skin. "I must take my leave," she continued, her voice now stiff. She darted her gaze to Liam. "It was nice to meet you, Lord MacLeod. Please tell your sister the same."

Before he could reply, she had hurried away.

Tarrymount looked to him. "Best to keep your distance from Miss Cartwright. She is not in the good graces of the *ton.*"

Irritation filled Liam. "I've always found that when warned away from a person, it makes me that more curious to know that person. Don't ye find that?" Liam turned on his heel, not bothering to wait for a reply. He had always liked puzzles that needed solving, and Miss Cartwright was quite the puzzle.

Three

The next afternoon, after haggling a good price for meat at the market, Cecelia stood in the narrow, shadowy aisle of Lexington Booksellers, running her finger down the spine of Byron's book of poetry.

Mr. Lexington cleared his throat, and when she glanced over her shoulder at him, his mouth twisted unpleasantly. "Miss Cartwright, if you are not going to purchase that book, please do not keep touching it."

Reluctantly, she withdrew her hand, but as she brought it to her side, a bolt of determination filled her. She reached up, snatched the book off the shelf, and marched up to the counter. She plunked it down before dour Mr. Lexington. "I would, in fact, like to purchase this book," she announced.

Mr. Lexington gave her a surprised look. "You wish to actually buy this book? *Today?*"

As the bell over the entrance behind her jingled to announce a new customer, embarrassment heated Cecelia's cheeks. She prayed that whoever it was would hurriedly pass by the front counter. The *clop clop* of shoes against the hardwood floor filled the quiet store, and blessedly, the newcomer seemed to move past the counter, but how far she was not certain as Mr. Lexington started talking again, overly loud. She cringed.

"Miss Cartwright, you did not answer me. Do you wish

to actually purchase this book today, or will this be like the many other times that you have come in here in the past year, handled my books, and then left without buying a thing?"

She glared at the odious man. If she had any money to spare, she most definitely would have bought some books. She was almost glad in this moment that she did not have the money, though, as Mr. Lexington was horrid and did not deserve her business. Still, her heart ached thinking of the ruined the book her father had paid good money to buy her. She wished to replace it, even though it would not be the one he had bought. Alas, she could not afford it.

She cleared her throat. "As soon as I acquire the funds I will give them to you. If you would please just hold this book for me." She eyed the only remaining copy of Byron's book.

"No," Mr. Lexington snapped, snatched the book from her hands, and scowled at her. "I suggest you go home."

"And I suggest ye learn to treat yer customers with more respect," came a cool, disapproving voice from directly behind her.

She knew that voice! Cecelia whirled around and looked up into Liam's face. His eyes, cold and filled with dislike, were fastened on Mr. Lexington.

Her heart skipped several beats at the sight of him. "Lord MacLeod!" she exclaimed. "Whatever are you doing here?"

His gaze softened on her. "I had a sudden, keen desire to purchase Lord Byron's book of poetry, *Hours of Idleness*."

Cecelia sucked in a sharp breath. Was that because of their encounter?

"You are in luck, my lord," Mr. Lexington said. Cecelia faced Mr. Lexington and frowned at him as he patted the book with a happy grin. "This is the last copy I have in stock."

As the bookseller told Liam the price and Liam produced the money, jealousy and slight resentment stirred in Cecelia. She had no right to begrudge Liam for having the funds to purchase the book. Even so, tears pricked her eyes, and she quickly moved away from the counter and started toward the door.

"Miss Cartwright!" Liam called after her. She pretended not to hear him, fearful that she could not hold back her tears of frustration and loss. Blinking rapidly, she rushed through the door and collided with Aila.

"Oh! I'm terribly sorry!" Cecelia said, reaching out to steady Aila, whom she had knocked into rather hard.

Aila waved her off with a smile. "I'm verra sturdy. A knock from a slight lady like ye is not likely to make me fall." Aila frowned. "Whatever is the matter? Ye look distressed."

Before Cecelia could answer, she heard the store door open behind her, and she knew, without turning, that it was Liam. She could sense it for some reason. Though it was more likely the smile of fondness that came to Aila's face that indicated his presence.

"What have ye there?" Aila asked him.

"I bought a book of Byron's poems...for Miss Cartwright."

Cecelia would have swooned if she were the swooning type. Slowly, she turned to face Liam. When their eyes met, she shivered at the seductive look he gave her. Or was she imagining that?

"You bought that book for me?" she fairly whispered. An eager light filled his eyes and made her heart squeeze.

"Aye. I could not get the picture of how sad ye looked

to have ruined yer father's gift out of my mind. I know it's improper, but I hope ye don't mind me doing such a thing."

Mind? She was so very touched and amazed, yet—"That is very kind of you. But I cannot possibly accept a gift from you, especially one so expensive," she said, unable to keep her eyes from wandering longingly to the book in his hands.

His eyes seemed to probe her very soul. "I'm sure a lady who is not like others of the *ton* would not let a few foolish social edicts stop her from accepting a gift she knows is harmless."

Cecelia stared at the book, which she had been in the habit of reading every night before bed since the day her father had given it to her. She swallowed hard, warring with herself. She desperately wanted to accept the gift. It *was* harmless. But to accept it *would* be improper, and not adhering to the rules of etiquette was exactly what had landed her in her current situation.

"Oh, for heaven's sake!" Aila exclaimed. She took the book from Liam's hands and thrust it at Cecelia. "Accept it, and consider it a gift from me, not my brother."

Cecelia acknowledged Aila's gesture with an inclination of her head, but she kept her gaze on Liam. "Can you afford such a gift?" When his eyes widened and he and his sister exchanged a swift look, Cecelia regretted her blunt question. "I beg your pardon. I should not have asked. It's just that I have heard of the struggles in the Highlands." And his sister had said he was *just barely* a lord.

Again, Liam and Aila exchanged a look, and as Aila opened her mouth, Liam shook his head at her. Had she been about to confess their clan's financial woes?

Liam smiled at Cecelia. "I appreciate yer concern. Please…let me do this for ye."

"His pride is involved now," Aila asserted.

"Oh!" Cecelia exclaimed. She feared if she did not take it, she would make him feel poorly about his likely lack of funds. She grasped the book Aila had been holding out to her and brought it close to her chest. "Thank you," she said, her voice catching on a swell of emotion that clogged her throat. "I'm not sure how I will ever repay you."

A devilish smile came to Liam's lips. "Ye can repay me by allowing me to escort ye wherever ye are going next."

Slowly, Cecelia nodded. "I am going to see my same friend as yesterday," she said.

As Liam held out his arm for Cecelia to take, Aila said, "And I still have a bit of shopping to do. Cecelia, it was nice to see ye again, and Liam, I will see ye back at the Rochburns'."

Cecelia did not miss the curious look Aila gave her brother, but before she could contemplate it further, Liam spoke. "Shall we?"

She nodded, took his arm, and tried to ignore the goose-flesh that raced across her skin the moment they touched. As they started down the street toward Elizabeth's, Cecelia felt she had to apologize for the way she had rushed away yesterday when Lord Tarrymount had appeared.

Stealing a glance at Liam, she said, "I'm terribly sorry if I seemed rude yesterday when Lord Tarrymount appeared. I, er, could not afford to linger and visit," she fibbed, hating herself for the lie. She held her breath with the fear that perhaps Lord Tarrymount had made mention of her disgrace and Liam would now know she was lying. Yet, if Lord Tarrymount had spoken ill of her, surely Liam would not be with her now.

He regarded her quizzically for a moment, and her belly clenched with the certainty that he knew of her disgrace.

"That's quite all right," he said, and she could not stop

the relieved exhalation that escaped her. "Tell me, Cecelia, besides reading Byron, what do ye like to do?"

She had the sudden, irrational desire to speak the truth and see if he looked at her with the wariness all men other than Blackmore always had. "I like to race horses. I like to take off my stockings and shoes, and feel the water on my feet. I like to laugh too loud and speak of politics." The more she confessed the faster her footsteps became. "I like to speak the truth, which has gotten me in a great amount of trouble in the past. I like to eat hearty meals, and basically, I like all manners of things a proper lady should not like. Or should not admit to liking, at least."

She stopped and was startled to realize they were already standing in front of Elizabeth's home. Cecelia carefully pulled her arm away from Liam's, feeling utterly foolish for her rant. Whatever had come over her? Whatever kept coming over her when this man was near? He was a stranger, yet he made her want to admit such personal things, things she ought not tell anyone.

She faced him and half expected him to be looking at her as if she were a raving madwoman. One corner of his mouth quirked up into an actual smile. He had a beautiful mouth.

"Ye're a verra interesting lady, Cecelia. Unlike anyone I've ever met."

"I'm sure I've horrified you," she asserted, clutching the book he had given her and turning her head away in embarrassment.

When his finger came under her chin, she let out a soft gasp. He made her look at him once more. "Ye have intrigued me, not horrified me. I assure ye."

She had no notion what to say to that, but her stomach fluttered with pleasure at his words. Just as a smile tugged at her mouth, Jonathan turned the corner to appear at the end of the street. She stiffened. She most definitely did not want to encounter that blackguard with Liam nearby where he could overhear the exchange.

Bobbing a quick curtsy, she blurted, "I must go!" She bit her lip at the surprised shock that swept across Liam's face, but over his shoulder, she could plainly see Jonathan's eyes narrowed upon her. Without wasting another moment, she rushed up the same steps she had yesterday and left Liam exactly where she had the previous day. If he had not thought her a lunatic before, he likely did now.

Her heart hammered as she knocked on Elizabeth's door, and she fairly barreled her way into the home when Elizabeth's ancient butler, Cooper, opened the door.

"Miss Cartwright, are you quite well?" he asked, his silver eyebrows arching.

Ignoring the butler for the moment, she rushed to a small window beside the door, pulled back the covering just a bit, peeked out of it, and felt her stomach clench as Jonathan passed by Liam without speaking. Clearly, they did not know each other. Liam stood on the walkway staring at the door for one more long moment before he turned away and departed.

Oh, she was most certainly not well. She had not been truly well in quite a long time, and she was starting to lose hope that she would ever be so again.

Behind her, Cooper loudly cleared his throat. Cecelia released the covering over the window, turned slowly to the butler, and offered him an apologetic smile. "I'm terribly sorry. I thought I saw someone I knew." She could not very well say she was avoiding one of the lying scoundrels responsible for her downfall and spying on him.

Cooper inclined his head, taking her excuse without so

much as the blink of an eye. "Lady Burton has been fretting that you were not going to be able to slip away to visit her today, since you are later than normal. She'll be so happy that you're here."

A large lump formed in Cecelia's throat. Elizabeth, though thirty-odd years older than Cecelia, had become her closest friend and confidant since Cecelia's father's ruination and then her own. When Father had died, Lady Burton had just been taking up residence in her London townhome. She had moved here from Yorkshire, where she said she had been summarily snubbed since her husband's death. Lonely, she had come to London hoping to meet people who had a more open attitude toward her past as an opera singer, yet she had found herself in the same predicament she had faced in Yorkshire. She was not considered "good enough" to befriend by those in the *ton* because she had one been an opera singer before she married, and she was looked upon skeptically and thought of as "too good" by those who came from a class similar to the one from which she hailed because she did have money thanks to her beloved husband.

Cecelia had soon found herself alone, too, and they had struck up a friendship until Mother had forbidden it, fearing that if anyone learned of the close acquaintance, it would make matters worse with the *ton*. Cecelia had not wanted to defy her mother's wishes and cause her more anxiety, but she did not want to give up her friendship with Elizabeth, either.

"Are you ready to proceed into the drawing room, Miss Cartwright?" the butler asked.

Cecelia blinked, realizing she had been lost in her thoughts. "Oh, dear me. Yes, Cooper. Thank you."

As they moved away from the front entrance, a fresh, piney scent hit Cecelia, followed by an earthier scent she recognized as rosemary. The rosemary stirred memories of happier times when Mother had insisted on decorating their house for Christmastide as her mother and her mother's mother always had. It was not fashionable to do so nowadays, but in that one instance, Mother had tilted her nose up to the de rigueur. No longer did her mother do this, of course. They did not have the money, nor did Mother have the spirit of cheer. Oh, how Cecelia wished this Christmastide she could give Mother a bit of her happiness back, and selfishly, Cecelia wished for a smidgeon of her own.

She cast her gaze around the entrance hall, searching for the source of the smells. To her delight rosemary and a plant that she did not recognize decorated the staircase banister. As Elizabeth had moved into this townhome after Christmastide last year, Cecelia did not know if decorating for the holiday season was a tradition for her or not. But today was the sixth day of December, and since Cecelia had been to Elizabeth's home yesterday—and the home had not had any greenery adorning it then—Cecelia suspected that the marchioness must also have the odd habit of decorating for Christmastide and had done it after Cecelia had departed the day before. However, these decorations were early and Mother would say they were bound to bring ill luck.

Cecelia followed Cooper's slow progress to the drawing room and gasped in delight at the transformation. Holly, laurel, and mistletoe hung above the doorway and along the mantle of the fireplace, and in the corner, the same greenery Cecelia did not recognize on the banister adorned the table. Elizabeth sat perched rather properly with a book in one hand, but her silver head of soft curls tilted scandalously back to sip on her Scotch—a practice Cecelia knew Elizabeth's husband had encouraged when he was alive—

hinting at how little regard the marchioness held for propriety.

Cecelia strolled into the room, her heart feeling immensely lighter, as it always did when she was here, in the company of someone who believed in her innocence.

She picked up a book of poems and sat in the chair Elizabeth always had waiting for her. Elizabeth lowered her glass and, with a conspiratorial look, slowly pushed a second crystal tumbler across the dark wood table toward Cecelia.

"I poured you a teensy, tiny sip," she said. Elizabeth grinned, her pale, wrinkly cheeks creasing even more, and her blue eyes sparking to life.

If Mother even knew Cecelia was at Elizabeth's home there would be the devil to pay, so if Mother knew Cecelia had indulged in a drink, *in the middle of the day*, she might very well ship her daughter off to the nearest convent. Ladies did not do such things, she thought as she curled her fingers around the cool glass. She was not the hoyden everyone painted her to be, but she understood deep within that she was not the prim-and-proper miss she knew she should be, either. This was her one secret, wicked indulgence in a life that had lost all color but boring, drab gray.

Cecelia brushed a finger across the dark, prickly green decorations. "What is this? I've never seen it."

"No?" Elizabeth asked in surprise, her French accent more pronounced than usual. Cecelia had learned that Elizabeth had left her family in Paris many years before when she married the Marquess of Burton. The union had been quite scandalous since Elizabeth had been an opera singer and had not been considered fit by the *ton* to be the wife of the marquess. She had been barely tolerated by Society, and when her husband had died, she had been no longer tolerated at all. Her distaste for societal rules was even greater than Cecelia's.

"This is evergreen," Elizabeth told her. "I put it here, especially for you."

"Me? Whatever for?"

Elizabeth smiled wickedly, as only a French woman of advanced years could. "In medieval times, it was thought to bring fertility. I once heard a story about a great medieval healer named Marion who had put evergreen throughout her home—Dunvegan Castle in Skye, I believe it was—so that she would conceive another son for her husband."

Cecelia's cheeks flamed instantly at the image of Liam that flashed in her mind. At Elizabeth's merry chuckle, Cecelia fanned herself and took a sip of her Scotch, which heated her further instead of cooling her.

"I don't need to be fertile," she whispered, certain that even though her mother was many townhomes away, she might somehow see Cecelia upon her return and know she had talked of improper things.

"Not now, you don't, dear," Elizabeth replied, "but you will when you marry!"

"But who would marry me?" she asked, voicing the concern she normally held deep within. "I'm disgraced in the *ton's* eyes, and even if I were not, I don't have anything to bring to a marriage."

Elizabeth took Cecelia's hand in her bony one. "Shh, my dear. You have yourself to bring to a marriage, and any man of any true value will recognize that your good heart and joyful, loyal spirit are worth more than a hundred bags of gold. Perhaps the Scot you told me of meeting yesterday?" she teased, raising her eyebrows.

Cecelia dashed a hand across her eyes, which had pooled with unshed tears. Purposely ignoring Elizabeth's comment about Liam, Cecelia asked, "Is that what happened with your husband?"

Elizabeth squeezed Cecelia's hand. "Yes, exactly. When George told his father he wanted to marry me, his father threatened to take away all money and property that was not entailed. George wisely told him to go to the devil and married me anyway." She winked at Cecelia.

Excited because she had heard the story before and it gave her hope, Cecelia could not help but finish it. "And because neither George nor his father had any siblings, he decided he could not afford to lose the affection of his one living relative, his son."

"Precisely," Elizabeth crowed.

Cecelia set down her glass and glanced out the window, surprised but delighted to see snowflakes falling against the graying sky. Unbidden, Aila MacLeod and her declaration that she was going to secure an invitation for Cecelia to the Rochburns' ball popped into Cecelia's head. "Perhaps this Christmastide season I will be allowed back into the *ton's* good graces, and I will meet a man who wishes to marry me, despite my circumstances."

The thought did not make her happy as it should.

Elizabeth patted Cecelia's hand. "Perhaps you will meet a man *not* of the *ton*, who cares naught for their rules and who does not believe the vicious gossip about you."

Cecelia knew Elizabeth was referring to Liam again. Sighing, she said, "You know I must try to secure a good match."

Elizabeth offered a scowl before she leaned to side of her chair—away from Cecelia—and seemed to be gathering something in her arms. When she straightened, she was holding wire, evergreen, apples, candles, and mistletoe.

"Whatever is all of that for?" Cecelia inquired.

"You could very well have a kiss stolen while standing

under this ball we are going to make," Elizabeth said in a conspiratorial voice.

"What?" Cecelia gasped. "From whom?"

"I suppose the Scot you just met, unless there is another gentleman vying for your attention."

Cecelia quickly shook her head. "There is no other. In truth, there is not even him. And I cannot afford to be fanciful."

"I will afford it for you, then," Elizabeth said on a harrumph. "I'm an old woman, and I suspect I don't have much longer to live."

Cecelia tsked at her friend. "Don't be ridiculous. You have years yet to enjoy. I'll make the ball with you, but I cannot take it home. I would have no way to explain it to Mama."

"Oh," Elizabeth said, frowning. "I hadn't thought of that. That's such a shame, as the only man ever in this house is Cooper, and I doubt you want a kiss from him."

"I shall pass," Cecelia said with a giggle.

For the next half hour, they worked on the ball as Elizabeth relayed a story about how her parents had first met at a party on Twelfth Night. Her father had found the bean in the Twelfth Night cake, which meant he got to pretend to be the king for the night, and her mother had found the pea, which meant she got to pretend to be the queen. They could each choose a partner they wanted to spend the night talking to, and they had chosen each other.

When the clock chimed two o'clock, Cecelia jumped up to leave. "I better hurry," she said, the continued heavy snowfall outside the window catching her attention.

"Miss Cartwright," Cooper interrupted as he appeared in the drawing room door. "There is a Lord MacLeod here who says he has come to escort you home."

Cecelia's heart leaped with excitement. "Where is he? The study?"

"Certainly not," the butler replied, his tone a protective one she had never heard before. "I was not about to let a stranger into this home without ensuring you know him and would like him to escort you home."

Cecelia frowned. "Do you mean to say you left him standing outside in the snow?"

"Of course I did," Cooper said with obvious pride.

"Cooper!" Elizabeth said, slowly rising to her feet, Cecelia assumed to scold her butler. "You are a genius!" Elizabeth crowed, motioning to him. "Make haste, my man, and secure the kissing ball over the front entranceway!"

Cecelia's mouth dropped open. When Cooper started walking toward the mistletoe ball to do Elizabeth's bidding, Cecelia gave herself a little shake. "Elizabeth, no! I do not even truly know Lord MacLeod."

"Pishposh," Elizabeth replied, brushing past Cecelia in a surprisingly spritely manner. Clearly, scheming put a spring in the woman's step. "I'm not suggesting anything indecent. It's customary, after all."

"Where?" Cecelia demanded. Her mother had never indulged in that particular custom.

"In my home," Elizabeth returned, and before Cecelia could protest further, Elizabeth was breezing out the parlor door while issuing orders to Cooper on how to quickly and correctly hang the kissing ball.

Cecelia actually had to double her step to try to catch up with Elizabeth, but by the time she reached her, Elizabeth was stepping around the chair Cooper had already managed to drag in front of the door, and her friend opened it—to Cecelia's great horror—just as Cooper announced triumphantly, "'Tis done, my lady. There was already a hook there."

As Elizabeth greeted Liam and introduced herself, she motioned him in while Cooper quickly moved the chair out of the way. Before Cecelia could even contemplate what to do, Liam filled the door, towering over her, Elizabeth, and Cooper, who stepped out of the way, and then turned and quit the entrance hall.

Liam reached up, his coat straining against his massive shoulders, and brushed the snow out of his hair. Cecelia had the sudden desire to sigh, but she managed to hold it in, even as wet tendrils of hair curled against his forehead, enhancing his appeal. He looked utterly, perfectly ruffled. And he had, Cecelia decided, the most beautifully proportioned body she had ever seen. The muscles of his long legs—slightly spread—bulged against his tan breeches, and she could see that his arms filled out his coat just as fully as his shoulders. She had only just noticed he did not have on a cravat when her eyes took on a will of their own and feasted on the exposed skin of his neck and the very top of his chest.

When Elizabeth coughed delicately, Cecelia wrenched her gaze to Liam's eyes, which danced with amusement. "I cannot abide the cravat," he offered. "I've tried, but I'm afraid this is as civilized as I get. Aila says ye can take the man out of the Highlands, but ye cannot take the Highlands out of the man. I hope my bare state does not offend ye."

"Not at all," she replied, fighting to keep from gawking at his chest once more. "Whatever are you doing here?"

His face, unfashionably bronzed by the sun yet achingly handsome, softened even as his burning eyes made her catch her breath. "I took a turn around the park after ye hurried away, and when it started to snow, it occurred to me that ye may verra well need assistance to yer home with the delicate slippers ye have on. I'd not be able to sleep tonight worried ye might take a fall again and not have anyone there to assist ye."

Her mouth parted with as much shock as pleasure. He'd been concerned for her?

She glanced at Elizabeth, who was grinning like a loon at Liam.

"I sh-should be going," Cecelia said slowly.

"Oh yes," Elizabeth agreed, so readily that suspicion shot through Cecelia just as Elizabeth gripped her by the arm and dragged her in front of Liam with shocking strength. "My goodness!" she exclaimed. "You two are standing under my Christmastide kissing ball!"

Liam's brow wrinkled. "Yer what?"

Cecelia could feel heat practically pouring off her body from embarrassment. "It's of no importance," she rushed out, which elicited a scowl from Elizabeth.

"The kissing ball is a tradition I uphold for Christmastide," the French woman explained.

Liam looked up at the ball, and Cecelia could see a distinctly skeptical expression cross his face. "We celebrate Hogmanay—the last day of the new year—in the Highlands," he offered as he turned his attention to them once more. A devilish smile curved his lips. "But if it's the tradition here to celebrate Christmastide—"

"It's not, truly!" Cecelia interjected, rubbing the burning tips of her ears.

"It is in my home," Elizabeth added.

Liam nodded at both women. "I certainly want to respect yer customs." He glanced at Cecelia. "Will ye do me the honor?"

A longing to kiss him shot through her, yet how could she? After all that had occurred, after how far she'd fallen—precipitated by the exuberant rule-snubbing behavior that had been trying to resurface since she had met this man—she *had* to be proper. She simply had to live a gray life. No more vivid colors of joy and spontaneity for her if she was to make amends with the *ton* and secure a safe future for herself and, in turn, her mother.

She swallowed, the noise resounding in her ears, and she licked her suddenly stiff lips. "We scarcely know each other," she whispered, the threads of her voice sounding regretful to her own ears.

"Aye, that's true enough," he agreed. "But I'm trying to remedy that." He cocked an eyebrow at her.

"Oh, you must share a kiss!" Elizabeth encouraged.

Cecelia glanced at her friend and could not help but laugh at the indignation and determination shining in Elizabeth's blue eyes.

"Will ye trust me?" Liam asked Cecelia, his gaze holding hers.

"That's quite a question, Lord MacLeod. I've trusted before and much regretted the foolish decision."

"Ah, but I'm a Scot, Miss Cartwright. My word is my honor. I will never break it."

She swallowed. "I daresay, it's hard to argue with such a declaration. You have my *temporary* trust. Now what are you going to do with it?"

"Give me yer hand," he replied in a voice that was but a velvet murmur, yet left room for nothing but compliance. He was, she understood in that instant, a man who was accustomed to being obeyed. And why would he not be? He had a presence about him that commanded acquiescence.

Slowly, she offered her gloved hand to him.

"Oh, dear me," Elizabeth exclaimed, making Cecelia jump and Liam turn to see what was the matter. "I do believe the snowfall grows even heavier!"

Cecelia watched as Elizabeth made her way across the entrance hall to the window farthest from them, though there was one much closer. "Yes," she murmured, without turning around. "It is falling in buckets now. I do so love to watch the snow." She kept her back squarely to Cecelia and Liam.

Cecelia loved her dear friend for attempting to give them a modicum of privacy while remaining in the room, as was proper.

Cecelia turned to Liam and was surprised to find him watching her. Something intense flared in his eyes as he reached for her hand and gently clasped it. Her heart pounded, and heat swirled within her chest. Slowly, he peeled off her glove, and when his warm skin came in contact with hers, her heart jolted and she had to stifle a gasp. Her eyes sought his, sure she did not have the effect on him that he had on her. But the smoldering flames she saw there startled her, then sent her spirits soaring.

He caressed her with his gaze as his fingers found their way to the tips of her own, grasped them in a sure hold, and raised them to his lips. As he brushed a kiss across her skin, everything about him consumed her. His heat enveloped her—most especially upon the top of her hand, which felt singed from his touch—her heart fluttered wildly when his warm breath washed over her sensitized skin, and her belly tingled. He brought her hand down between them, and much to her surprise, he began to put her glove back on her with such tender care that she shivered. Desire unlike any she had ever known ran through her.

When he was done, he released her, but neither of them moved. They stood face-to-face, and she could almost feel a connection forming between them.

Jonathan had kissed her on the lips before, but his kiss

had elicited nothing in her. It was a gray, drab exchange. But a single kiss upon her hand from Liam had sent her senses swirling as if she'd just watched the most magnificent display of colorful fireworks in the sky. His eyes, she realized, were on her mouth, and she had the overwhelming urge to press her lips to his.

She forced herself to step back. "I need to be making my way home," she said.

He nodded. "Of course."

After she collected her new book and they said their farewells to Elizabeth, they stepped outside. A cold breeze whipped Cecelia's hair up around her neck, and she wrapped her arms around her middle to ward off the chill. She had been rushing to leave the house this morning, knowing she had wanted to go by the bookstore after the market, and she had not taken the time to don a pelisse.

As they descended the steps away from Elizabeth's home, Liam paused, so Cecelia did as well. When she looked to question him, he had removed his coat. He arched an eyebrow at her.

"May I?" he asked, as he jangled the coat a bit.

She nodded and stood, unmoving, as he placed his coat over her shoulders. She was immediately enveloped in his lingering warmth and masculine scent. She felt utterly drugged. She was not the hoyden they said she was, she reminded herself, but she *could* suddenly see how a woman might be led down a less than virtuous path by a man such as Liam. He had a lure about him unlike anything she had ever encountered before. In truth, it scared her a little. She could not afford to be foolish, yet it was hard to think sensibly with him near.

He took her hand to help her down the last step, and as he did, Lord Northington, one of Jonathan's friends, appeared around the corner. He paused when he saw them, and then a distinct leer spread across his face. She stiffened and immediately released Liam's hand. Lord Northington was not the first man to leer at her. Since Jonathan and Lord Tarrymount had conspired to ruin her, she had been subjected to the most lurid offers the few times she had been out in Society. Frankly, she had almost been relieved when invitations to events hosted by the *ton* had stopped arriving.

Lord Northington tipped his hat to them and then strode by with a chuckle. Embarrassment churned in her stomach. She turned her head away, praying the cool air would lessen the redness she was sure marked her cheeks. Behind her, she heard Liam shift. She had to turn around, she had to explain, but words failed her. How could she explain her disgrace to a man she hardly knew? She was trying to work it out in her head when a horrific notion hit her.

She faced Liam and found pity in his eyes. Knots filled her stomach. Lord Tarrymount must have mentioned something already for Liam to look at her so. She simply had to know.

"Did Lord Tarrymount say anything about me to you?"

He did not answer right away, but he did not need to. Wariness crept into his eyes, and her heart crashed to her feet.

"He did," Liam said, hesitating as if he was taking her measure, or perhaps deciding if he would say more.

She barely resisted the urge to press her hands over her ears as humiliation crashed over her, followed swiftly by anger. She stared at the beautiful man before her. She was a blithering idiot. Feathers for brains, that's what she had. Had he thought her a woman of easy virtue and, therefore, intended to pursue her? That made much more sense than him having a genuine interest in her.

"I see," she finally replied, though her words were jerky and stiff. "I hate to disappoint you, Lord MacLeod—"

"Liam," he reminded her with an easy smile that simultaneously made her chest squeeze and infuriated her. How could he affect her so? She had only just met him, *and* he had proven to be a blackguard!

"Lord MacLeod," she said, perfectly aware she sounded like a shrill shrew, "I am not interested in a romp, contrary to what you must have been told and obviously believe."

His eyes narrowed and his nostrils flared as she shrugged out of his coat and threw it toward him, then turned on her heel and quickly marched away.

For a moment, all was silent behind her, and then his footsteps were approaching quickly. She hurried onward, determined to reach her house and the sanctuary it offered. Just as she made it to her front steps, her foot slipped on a slick patch of ice—again—and she careened backward. Liam caught her and pulled her against his hard chest, then set her gently away and turned her around.

There was a lethal calmness in his gaze, yet she could see his jaw twitching. He was angry. He tugged a hand through his hair, then spoke. "I do not think ye are interested in a romp, Cecelia."

"B-but Lord Tarrymount—" she sputtered.

"Warned me to stay away from ye because of some nonsense about not being in the good graces of the *ton*."

"Oh dear," she mumbled, horrified at how she had acted. Before she could say more, the door opened and her mother stood there gaping at her.

"Cecelia!" Mother gasped, looking between her and Liam. "Where have you been?"

"The market took longer than I expected," Cecelia lied, hiding her book behind her back and shooting Liam a pleading look. A frown appeared between his brows, but he did not refute her story. "I almost fell on the ice, and Lord MacLeod here caught me." Never mind that it had happened yesterday, too.

The glare on her mother's face instantly disappeared, and a smile took its place. "*Lord* MacLeod, you say?"

Cecelia nodded as dread settled in her stomach. She knew how much her mother wanted her to make a good match. Once she realized Liam was not wealthy, however, Cecelia feared the worst.

"Where are you from, Lord MacLeod?" Mother demanded. "I don't recognize your name."

"The Isle of Skye, Lady…?"

"Oh dear me!" Cecelia cried out. "Lord MacLeod, might I present my mother, Lady Thornberry. Mama, as I'm sure you have gathered, this is Lord MacLeod."

"Has your clan been greatly affected as most others?" Mother asked to Cecelia's mortification, ignoring her daughter and going straight to the topic that interested her most—whether or not Liam had any money.

Liam nodded, and Mother's friendly smile disappeared. Her lips pressed together as Cecelia had feared. "I see," she replied curtly. "I am terribly sorry about that. Cecelia!" Mother's sharp voice made Cecelia cringe. "Hurry inside before you catch a chill."

With how hot her mortification was making her, Cecelia was positive catching a chill was not a worry she needed to consider. She offered Liam an apologetic look. "I'm awfully sorry about earlier, and well—" She shrugged and cast a helpless look toward her mother—"everything. Please," she said, lowering her voice as her mother turned to go inside, "don't judge my mother too harshly. She has not always been so—"

"Friendly and welcoming to strangers?" Liam supplied with a wink.

Cecelia had to smother her laugh. "You are very kind," she whispered. He could have been angry at her mother's dismissal of him based solely on her discovery that he was not a catch, yet he was generous about her less than charitable attitude.

"Cecelia!" Mother called, her tone impatient. "Now, if you please."

She didn't please, not at all. She wished to linger for a moment more and stare into Liam's beautiful eyes, which seemed to look upon her without judgment. But with a farewell wave of her hand, she turned dutifully toward the gray door. She did not have the luxury of falling for a gentleman like Liam, however wonderful he seemed.

Four

Liam strolled back to the Rochburns' thinking about Cecelia and her accusation that he had thought she wished for a romp because Lord Tarrymount had said something to him. So Cecelia not being in the *ton's* good graces had something to do with a gentleman, or perhaps with her having been perceived unfairly after likely failing to behave exactly as the *ton* deemed proper. From what he had seen of the *ton* so far, it seemed to be made up of pretentious, judgmental, vain people with too much money and not enough heart.

He nodded to the butler as the man opened the door, and then he strolled through the entrance hall, intending to find Aila and see if she had managed to secure Cecelia an invitation to the ball. He wanted to see her again and spend more time with her, but her mother's cold attitude toward him made him certain he would not be welcome to call there. That left the ball. At such an occasion, he could dance with her and possibly speak to her alone again in a quiet corner.

He started to make his way toward the stairs to Aila's room but paused when he saw his sister hunkered over with her ear pressed to the drawing room door. Chuckling softly, he quietly went to her and tapped her on the shoulder. With a jerk and a gasp, Aila stood so fast she nearly knocked him on the chin with her head.

She stepped back and to the side, and scowled up at him. "Ye gave me a fright!" she accused in a whisper.

He smirked. "Ye'd not be in the position to be frightened if ye were not eavesdropping at a door. What is it ye're trying to hear?" As the question left his mouth, a distinctly feminine, distinctly irate voice rose from within the study and drifted toward them in murmured, indistinguishable words. A louder, clearer male voice followed. It belonged to Aila's betrothed.

Aila pressed a finger to her lips and leaned forward as if to hear what Aldridge would say, but the gesture was not necessary. He fairly bellowed at his mother. "Aila has made a friendship! It is her first here in England, and she is joyful because of it. I will not have you ruining her happiness with your harsh judgment of Miss Cartwright!"

"Harsh judgment?" the duchess exclaimed. "I saw it with my own eyes. Right here in our home!"

"Enough, Mother!" Aldridge thundered at the same time another male voice, deeper and laced with even more irritation than Aldridge's had been, chimed in.

"Penelope," the man—it had to be the Duke of Rochburn, Aldridge's father—said in a gruff tone. "I have sat back and said nothing as you joined the ranks of busybodies that passed judgment on that young lady, but I'll not sit silent now and watch as you drive Aldridge away."

"I would never drive Aldridge away!" the duchess exclaimed.

"Not intentionally, my dear, but unintentionally…"

A loud sniff came from within, which Liam assumed was the duchess displaying her wounded feelings.

"Our son," the duke continued without commenting on his wife's sniffling, "has only just returned from a war I let him leave for with anger between us, and now that God has seen fit to bring him home to us, and with a lovely woman he wishes to wed, I'll not let you cause more anger and division in our family. I have learned my lesson, and you should, too."

"I'm not a child to be scolded, Rochburn!" the duchess wailed as a child would.

Liam and Aila exchanged an amused look.

"I will cease the scolding when you cease acting like a child," the duke replied to his wife's declaration in a stern tone. "Miss Cartwright will receive an invitation to the ball because it will please Aldridge's bride-to-be and therefore our son, which will please me. I daresay the young lady has learned her lesson, if there ever was one to teach her. I for one, am not certain there was."

Silence reigned for a minute, and Liam and Aila exchanged a long look. Whatever had occurred with Cecelia, it seemed she had at least two men who championed her.

"I'll do as you command," the duchess said in a dramatic tone, "but don't blame me if the *ton* snubs your betrothed because of her choice in friends."

"I'm positive, Aila will manage the snub, *if* she should receive it. She is a Scot and, therefore, has a backbone of steel."

Liam grinned at Aila. "I like him," he whispered to his sister.

She nodded as the duchess spoke again. "I better go see about the invitation, then," the duchess said with a sigh.

"Excellent, Mother."

"You should tell Aila about Miss Cartwright, though, so that she is prepared to be snubbed."

"I do not believe anyone would dare," Aldridge countered. "They all know if they did such a thing, they'd have to face you, and are you not the Ice Duchess?"

Liam had heard enough. Cecelia was going to be invited to the ball, and that was what mattered to him. And from what Aldridge had said, it seemed that what had occurred with Cecelia had been overblown. Liam took Aila by the arm and guided her upstairs to her bedchamber where they might talk in private. Once the door was shut, they faced each other.

Aila quirked her lips, as was her habit when she was contemplating something. "What do ye suppose occurred with Cecelia?"

He shrugged. "I've no notion. Why would I?"

Aila smirked at him. "Well ye did insist we go to that bookstore today for ye to buy her a book, and then ye did have time alone with her, did ye not?"

"I did," he agreed, not ready to speak of what he and Cecelia had discussed.

Aila's smirk deepened. "I've never known ye to buy anything for a lass, or be concerned for one. Other than when she is trying to trap ye into marrying her, that is."

He scowled at his sister. "That's true enough, but I am not worried that Cecelia is trying to trap me into marriage."

"Because she has no notion ye have money and land," Aila said flippantly.

"Aye," he replied.

Aila's gaze locked with his. "Why did ye not correct her erroneous belief?"

"Because it is nice to be able to get to know someone and judge her reaction to me based solely on who I am. Can ye understand?"

"I can." His sister studied him. "Do ye wish me to ask Richard exactly what occurred with her, so ye may be properly informed before perusing her further?"

He shook his head. "If there is a tale about her to be told, I'd rather get it from her lips."

Aila grinned and hugged him. "I knew ye would say that! I cannot wait for the ball tomorrow night! I'm more excited for ye than for myself."

He usually did not care for large social gatherings where he would have to spend a good portion of his time avoiding scheming lasses, but Cecelia would hopefully be there, and she'd not be scheming to get him. He found the prospect very appealing.

The next night, the Rochburns' ballroom buzzed with hundreds of guests, but Liam was only concerned about one—Cecelia. An hour into the party to celebrate Aila and Aldridge's betrothal, Cecelia still had not made an appearance. As Liam stood by a column with a champagne flute in his hand and a scowl firmly on his face—to ward off the marriage-minded mamas who kept casting hopeful glances his way—his patience was wearing thin. His mood darkened as he began to suspect Cecelia was not going to come. The only question was why.

As he contemplated this, he watched a mother take hold of her daughter's arm and stride toward him with purposeful steps. She whispered in her daughter's ear, and by the time they reached him, both mother and daughter had matching gleams in their eyes. He did not doubt that their interest in him lay in his land and money and not at all in who he truly was.

The mother and daughter gave him coquettish smiles. "Lord MacLeod, we met you the first day you arrived in London," the mother said. "I'm sure you recall."

He honestly did not, but he nodded, not wishing to injure their sensibilities.

"This is my daughter, Francis. She is a lovely dancer."

"I'm certain she is," he replied, looking beyond the women toward the entrance in the hope of seeing Cecelia. The mother before him made him think of Cecelia's mother, who had clearly dismissed him the moment she had thought him without wealth. Cecelia had seemed embarrassed by her mother's behavior, and his instinct told him that Cecelia was different.

Just as the thought entered his mind, she appeared like a vison from a fantasy, encased in a white silk gown that made her look rather like a snow fairy. Her black hair was piled on top of her head with tendrils of curls clinging to her creamy neck. He followed the expanse of beautiful, inviting skin down to the swell of her chest, which was modestly covered with white lace, and his blood heated. Her large brown eyes shone from her delicate face. She appeared defiant yet nervous at the same time. The contradiction was fascinating. She was the most beguiling creature he had ever beheld.

He stepped toward her, as if pulled by an invisible string, when a hand came to rest upon his arm. Annoyed, he looked to his right and into Francis's disbelieving face and her mother's annoyed one. Devil take it. He had completely forgotten the women beside him, lost as he was to the spell Cecelia cast over him without trying.

"Lord MacLeod, did you hear me?" the mother asked.

"I'm sorry to say I did not. Would ye mind repeating it, Lady…?" There was no hope to hide that he did not remember her name.

"Lady Dentington," she said, her voice pinched. "I said, Francis would be perfectly thrilled to dance with you, unless you do not care to do so." The woman arched her eyebrow all the way to her hairline.

Lady Dentington had cornered him, and he was the clot-heid who'd let her. He was certain that she had overstepped the social customs of London by being so bold, but he was also certain that she did not care. Sometimes being honorable was troublesome, and this was assuredly one of those times. He clenched his teeth as he extended a hand to Francis. He knew from Cecelia that it was not the English custom to refer to one another by their Christian names, but apparently when a mother was determined to catch a man for her daughter, etiquette was disposable.

As Francis took his hand, he sought out Cecelia once more. Where was she? She had moved from the entrance. The notes of the dance started, and he maneuvered Francis to the dance floor as he continued his search for Cecelia. On the first turn, while half listening to Francis chatter on about all the things she was more than capable of—such as enduring, without complaint, the cold Highland winter on the *barbaric* Isle of Skye—he found Cecelia in another man's arms.

He narrowed his gaze upon them. He was acquainted with Lord Egerton. Liam had not liked the man upon meeting him, and he liked him even less in this moment as his hand pressed into Cecelia's back. Liam noted her eyes first widen, then narrow. He thought seriously upon striding across the ballroom and wrenching the man's hand off her and possibly giving him a nice, hard jab in his overly long nose, but that would likely make the fools of the *ton* talk more about Cecelia. He did not want to do anything to harm her, but if that man's hand moved any lower…

Suddenly, Cecelia stepped away from Lord Egerton, said something, and then turned and moved off the dance floor with her head held high in a display of pride that made Liam want to grin.

As soon as the dance ended, he delivered Francis to her mother and started toward Cecelia. As he closed the distance, he watched her and her mother exchange what appeared to be words of disagreement, given their strained faces, and then another gentleman was in front of Cecelia and off she went again toward the dance floor as Liam weaved in and out of guests to get closer to her. When she next came off the dance floor he was going to intercept her.

He leaned against a column by a potted plant, and when another mother looked his way, he scowled, not feeling a hint of remorse when he noted her indignant gasp. Behind him, he heard a rustle, and as he looked to see who it was, his sister stepped up beside him.

"I've been watching ye," Aila said in a teasing voice.

"Are ye not supposed to be mingling with all the ladies and gentlemen ye will be living among?"

Aila shrugged. "Watching ye watch Cecelia is much more fun. I've never seen ye besotted."

"I am not besotted," he growled, though he suspected he could very well be, if he allowed himself to be. "I'm intrigued. There's a difference."

"Ye look besotted," Aila continued. "Why do ye not ask her to dance?"

"There has not been a chance," he replied, a tick starting in his jaw as Cecelia's current partner moved his hand dangerously low on her back. "Aila, I may have to hit a man this night. Will ye be angry?"

His sister turned her gaze from him to where Cecelia was dancing, and her mouth thinned. "I'd not be angry, but ye may want to try simply cutting in first. It would cause less tongues to wag, and I have a feeling Cecelia would appreciate that."

He nodded, and though he wanted to stride right onto the middle of the floor, he waited for Cecelia and her partner to move closer to the edge so he could intercede as discreetly as possible. Luckily, the room was so crowded that it would not be too noticeable when he did cut in. When they got so near that he could have touched Cecelia's sleeve, he did. She turned her head toward him, and the delight that crossed her face made his chest tighten.

"Miss Cartwright," he said, "I believe this was to be our dance."

"Oh yes!" she exclaimed, giving him a look of pure gratitude. "Lord Reeves, I am terribly sorry, but I forgot I promised this dance to Lord MacLeod." Cecelia stepped away from the man, who reached out as if he was going to grab her.

Liam immediately moved between them and turned his gaze on Lord Reeves. "Ye'll excuse us," he said, barely controlling his anger. Perhaps the depth of his brewing ire could be heard in his tone or seen on his face, for Lord Reeves shuffled backward with a nod.

"Of course," the man said.

As Lord Reeves moved away, Liam took Cecelia by the hand and brought her into the circle of his arms. Without a word, he moved them away from his grinning sister, marveling at the way Cecelia stirred desire in him by simply being near.

She tilted her head up and gazed at him with her dark, enthralling eyes. "Thank you," she said softly. "I was most uncomfortable and was trying to think how to end the dance."

"I could see ye were," he replied. "In this dance and the last."

Her eyes widened. "You were watching me?"

He'd not meant to admit that, but now that he had, he nodded, refusing to lie about it. "I was. I'd been hoping ye would come to the ball, and when ye appeared, I could not take my eyes from ye."

A grin appeared on her face, but it quickly faded. Her dark lashes fell to hide her gaze, and then they rose once more. Embarrassment shone in her eyes as her cheeks pinked.

"I saw those two men fail to give ye the respect ye deserve," he commented, guessing that was what was causing her obvious shame. He felt her tense under his fingertips. He considered abandoning his desire to know why she danced with the men, but he found he had to know.

"Why would ye agree to partner with such men?" he asked.

Her eyes darted to her right where her mother stood glaring at them, and then she turned her gaze back to his. Something dwelled there that looked suspiciously like regret. "One is a marquess, and the other is a viscount. Mama insisted."

He had thought perhaps that was the case, yet he needed to be certain. "Ye don't seem happy that such eligible gentlemen asked ye to dance."

Anger swept over her face, which surprised him. "Those men, like most everyone else in the *ton*, clearly think I have no morals. I warned Mama, but she refuses to hear it. She is determined that I marry well." As soon as the words flew from her mouth, she gasped. "I am sorry. I don't know what came over me to have said something so blunt. I always vow to be proper, but every time I'm with you, I seem to forget that vow."

When she moved as if to pull away, he gripped her

more tightly. "Please don't. I like that ye speak plainly, and I don't believe for a moment that ye have loose morals."

"You might if you knew what happened." The despair in her voice made him angry on her behalf and ignited a wish to protect her. It was strange to feel such a thing for someone he hardly knew, yet he did and could not explain it.

"Tell me, then," he said softly.

She turned her head away and spoke slowly. "I was caught in the arms of a man who was kissing me…a man who was not my betrothed."

He frowned. He could not imagine her being untrue. "There must be more to the story than that," he urged.

When her eyes met his, he could see the shock in them. "Do you know you are the first person to acknowledge that I might not have willingly kissed another? Even my own mother—" She bit her lip. "Well, I daresay, she thought I had a hand in my downfall, but I likely gave her reason to think so. Everyone, really. You see, I was not very good at following the rules of Society as a proper young lady should. I have always laughed too loud, raced horses when I ought not."

"Shocking," he teased, thinking upon his own sister who had always done such things, as well.

Cecelia gave him a perplexed look, as if trying to decide if he truly thought it was shocking or if he was goading her. "I once took off my shoes and stockings and frolicked in the waters of the Serpentine with a gentleman friend." She looked at him as if expecting him to run.

He barely resisted the urge to draw her near and kiss her. This woman did not have loose morals. She had a love for life that was too great for the stuffy confines of London. "I'm envious," he said in a low voice that throbbed with clear desire.

Her lips parted, and she inhaled a sharp breath. "Oh my," she finally murmured as the music ended. They stood there, unmoving. "You are quite surprising."

"As are ye."

"Cecelia!" Her mother's shrill voice bludgeoned Liam's eardrums. He and Cecelia looked at once toward the lady.

Cecelia let out a long sigh. "Mama."

"It's time to depart," Lady Thornberry said. "I have a megrim."

Disappointment besieged Liam when Cecelia nodded, though he could tell it was reluctantly so by the look she gave him.

"Go along and say your farewells to our hosts, Cecelia," her mother added. "I will follow."

Cecelia frowned but moved to do as she was bid. "Good night, Lord MacLeod. Perhaps we shall see each other again soon."

"I think not," her mother answered before he could. The woman was a giant splinter in his thumb; however, she was Cecelia's mother so he held his tongue.

The moment Cecelia was gone, her mother turned to him. "Lord MacLeod, might I be blunt?"

"By all means," he replied, feeling sure that even if he had said no, she would have done as she pleased anyway.

"My daughter is not for you. Please turn your attention elsewhere."

He suspected Cecelia's mother was saying this because she thought him lacking in funds, and she had apparently not yet been enlightened. He could tell her so now, but he wanted a bit more time to get to know Cecelia without the trappings that came with his status being known.

Lady Thornberry gave him an expectant stare, and he

knew she wished him to consent. That he could not do. Instead, he said, "How do ye know yer daughter and I would not suit? We've only just met. I daresay, neither of us even knows it."

"I know it," she snapped, "and Cecelia will do as I say. She owes it to me." With that, Lady Thornberry left him and disappeared into the thick crowd.

Suddenly, Aila was standing by his side. "I could not help but overhear," she said, giving him a concerned look.

"Ye mean ye were lurking and listening when ye ought not have been?"

Aila scowled. "That is a matter of perspective, brother dear. I am happy and in love, and I want to see ye the same." She plucked her hands on her hips, which meant she was about to give one of her lectures, which was highly amusing since he was laird. "Ye could make things much easier for yerself with Cecelia's mother by telling her that ye are wealthy."

"I could," he replied evenly, "but I prefer to know for certain that Cecelia likes *me*, despite her thinking I have nothing to offer other than myself."

Aila grinned. "Just as Father did to Mother!"

Liam nodded. "And Grandfather did to Grandmother."

She quirked her mouth. "How far back do ye think the tradition goes?"

He shrugged. "I'm uncertain."

"Ye'd not be the first laird to take an English bride. Remember the story of Lady Marion, and how our ancestor Iain married her to help save the king?"

"I remember," he said, chuckling, "but no one has said anything about me taking an English bride. I just met Cecelia."

"I know," Aila replied, but he could see the dreamy look

in her eyes. It was the same one she got whenever she talked about Aldridge. "But I see something between the two of ye. Some spark I've never seen with ye and any lass before."

He felt it, too, but he didn't say so. He knew better than to encourage his sister. She had a tendency to mettle when she should not, and her meddling had a habit of bringing confusion and chaos instead of clarification and order.

"Will ye call upon her?" she asked.

"I'd like to, but I don't think her mother will welcome it."

"I've an idea for that," Aila said, motioning to someone. Liam turned to find Aldridge headed toward them.

The marquess stopped in front of them, nodded congenially to Liam, and then smiled at Aila with obvious adoration. "I've been looking for you."

"Ye found me," she replied, slipping her arm into the crook of her betrothed's. "I've a favor to ask."

"Aila," Liam said, suddenly sure it had something to do with him and equally sure he did not want her dragging Aldridge into his personal matters.

Aila pointedly ignored him. "Liam would like to become better acquainted with Miss Cartwright—"

"For God's sake, Aila!" Liam growled.

She scowled at him, and Aldridge narrowed his eyes in Liam's direction, which actually pleased him. He was glad, indeed, that the man had a natural instinct to protect Aila, though she certainly needed no protection from Liam.

"Shh," Aila hissed. "Ye stubborn oaf! Richard, Miss Cartwright's mother believes Liam to be poor; therefore, she will not be open to Liam courting her daughter."

Aldridge gave Liam an amused look. "Do you wish to court Miss Cartwright?"

Did he? He thought he might, but he didn't intend to stand here discussing it. "Perhaps," was all he was willing to say.

"Why do you not tell Lady Thornberry and Miss Cartwright the truth?" Aldridge asked.

"The same reason ye led me to believe ye were a poor commoner, Richard," Aila said in a chiding voice.

Liam scowled. "Ye lied to my sister?"

"I did not lie," Aldridge rebutted, looking offended. "I merely did not correct her assumption about my person. 'Tis different."

Liam was about to argue that it wasn't, but in doing so, he would be diminishing the strength of his own reasoning, so he nodded his agreement.

Aila snorted. "And they say women are the schemers..."

Liam and Aldridge exchanged an amused, guilty look.

"I had grown tired of being chased because I was going to be a duke someday," Aldridge said.

"And I, a laird," Liam added.

Aldridge nodded. "In Scotland, I saw the perfect opportunity to reinvent myself, so to speak, when I met your sister."

Liam immediately thought of Cecelia. "I understand."

"What do you need me to do, MacLeod?" Aldridge asked.

"He needs ye to come up with a way to get Miss Cartwright out of her home with her mother's approval, so that he may have a chance to spend time with her. Perhaps ice-skating on the Serpentine," Aila suggested triumphantly.

"You clever, clever lady," Aldridge said with pride. "I can go in two days. I have business to attend to for the next day that will keep me rather tied up."

Two days seemed like an eternity, but with no other

option, Liam nodded his agreement.

Five

Cecelia could still scarcely believe she was sitting beside Liam, but as Aldridge's carriage hit a hard bump and Liam shot a hand out to steady her, she knew it was not just another lovely dream. His touch even lingered for a moment before disappearing. Over the past two nights, she had dreamed only of him. And oh, what dreams they had been! But after enduring her mother's lecture directly after the ball about why Cecelia could not encourage Liam's attention—and her own surety that Liam would never call on her after the way her mother had treated him—Cecelia had been positive she would never see him again.

In addition, Cooper's granddaughter, who worked at the Rochburns' home, had told Elizabeth's butler that Liam was planning to return to Scotland soon. When Elizabeth had mentioned it, Cecelia had felt such a wave of loss that she had made a hasty excuse to go home, where she spent the rest of the afternoon staring up at the ceiling in her bedchamber, silently bemoaning her fate.

This morning, when there had been a knock at their door and she had heard his voice, she had been certain she was imagining it, but when she glanced down the stairs, he'd been standing there beside his sister and Aldridge. Aila had inquired if Cecelia could join them in ice-skating, and Cecelia had held her breath in fear that her mother would say no. But when Aldridge had commented that he would watch over her, as he and several of his friends were also going—in particular, the Duke of Blackmore—Cecelia had known that Mother would allow her to attend.

Mother had never truly given up hope that Blackmore would one day realize he wished to marry Cecelia. Her mother knew very well that Blackmore had talked her into racing horses in Hyde Park, and that he had convinced her to remove her stockings and shoes to wade in the water of the Serpentine, but apparently Blackmore had now been forgiven by her mother. He was a duke, after all. Mother had been livid when Blackmore had not appeared to offer for Cecelia's hand when the whispers had started after they had frolicked in the water, but what her mother did not know was that Blackmore *had* offered and Cecelia had declined. She had not felt a special spark for him, but simply thought of him as a good friend. Yet, had she known how much damage those choices would cause, she might have accepted his offer purely to ease her parents' burden and the worries that came later. But she had not known, and when her father's gambling problem first came to light and they had ordered her to accept Jonathan's marriage proposal, Blackmore had long departed London, having defied his father's wishes, as Aldridge had his father's, and gone off to fight Napoleon. She had been glad for Blackmore, though, never begrudging or angry.

Cecelia stole a glance at Liam to find him assessing her. Her heart skipped several beats. She liked him very much. He made her feel something she had never experienced in her life—a strange stirring in the pit of her stomach, a rush of heat through her blood, a tightening in her chest, and delicious pinpricks across her skin. She thought perhaps he might find her intriguing, as well. He had said she was surprising, had kissed her hand so tenderly, and had told her he believed in her.

A smile tugged at his lips, and she could not help but return it. Still, she lowered her gaze, almost fearing the intense feelings he caused in her. She stared at his large, strong hands, which looked as if they could protect her from anything, but she knew well that looks were deceiving. Jonathan had looked harmless, yet he had inflicted great harm. And Liam, for all the strength he appeared to possess, would not be able to protect her from the guilt that would likely kill her if she did not secure a good match that allowed her mother to avoid living in poverty.

The unfairness of it all made Cecelia's stomach ache. She should not have come today! She had known Liam such a short time, yet she already mourned the loss of what might have been. Preposterous! Mayhap today she would find they would not have suited at all and she could rid herself of the sadness.

An hour later, swishing along the ice with the cool air blowing against her face, Cecelia pumped her legs as hard as she could in an effort to beat Liam to their designated finishing spot. When she reached it before him, she threw up her arms in victory while giving a very unladylike shout of joy and doing a twirl to show off her skills. It was the twirl that did her in. Her left skate slid away from her and down she went, straight into Liam's waiting arms.

His arms encircled her and pulled her, gently and tightly, against his hard chest. As she grasped him to steady herself and her fingers gripped his arms of steel, she turned her face to his to thank him. Green, probing eyes met hers, and her breath caught in her throat. Today would not be the day that she learned he did not suit her. Every moment with him led her to discover more about him that suited her perfectly.

"You seem to always be there to save me," she murmured, feeling drugged by his masculinity and nearness.

"I'm glad of it. What man would not wish to save such a lovely lass as yerself?" he replied in a deep tone that made heat pool in her belly. He reached out and tucked a strand of her hair behind her ear. "Ye look bonny with yer cheeks all red and yer lips so rosy."

She could feel his eyes raking over her mouth, and she was filled with a desire to know how he would kiss. Would it be perfect like the kiss she had always dreamed of receiving that would steal her breath and her senses, and send her heartbeat soaring? In that instant, she realized they were quite hidden from the view of the other skaters, and he could easily steal a kiss if he wanted to do so. His eyes took on a predatory gleam, and she knew he realized it, too.

An ache of longing coursed through her, so strong that it shocked and frightened her. She could not let him kiss her. She feared that if she did, her resolve to do what was needed would be permanently lost.

She pushed out of his arms, his eyes widening in surprise. "I'm very thirsty. And cold," she added, though she was blazing hot from her wanting of his lips on hers.

"I can take care of both those things," he said, and she was awfully glad he was not going to pursue stealing a kiss, nor question her abrupt shoving out of his arms.

He held his hand out to her, and she looked at it, debating with herself. She wanted very much to take his hand, but it was probably best not to indulge in such an intimacy when she knew perfectly well she could not allow it to go further. Yet, heaven help her, she reached out and grasped his hand anyway.

"Just for steadiness's sake," she said, praying he would not refute her excuse.

"Of course," he replied smoothly, though she vowed a look of triumph had flared in the depths of his eyes.

They skated hand in hand to the side of the bank, and then Liam encircled her waist with his arms. She gave him a questioning look, to which he replied, "Only to steady ye. I'd not wish to see ye fall and hurt yerself."

"Oh yes!" she agreed enthusiastically, then winced at just how keen she had sounded about having his hands upon her.

Once they were both off the ice, Liam led them to their shoes, his hands releasing her waist. One hand remained lightly on the small of her back to guide her. She had never felt so possessed in her life, nor more aware of how dangerous this man was to her. He was not a danger physically, of course. She knew instinctually that he would not lay a finger on her without her express consent. Too much honor radiated from him. No, her heart was in danger of being stolen by him, or perhaps simply *lost* to him. It would most definitely be broken if she was foolish enough to lose it to him.

I must not be foolish.

She repeated the mantra as she took off her skates, put on her shoes, and followed him to the carriage where they had left a basket of food and hot chocolate.

"Should we wait on Aila and Lord Aldridge before we indulge in a bit of the fare Lord Aldridge's cook sent with us?" she asked.

Liam glanced toward the ice and shook his head. "I think they will likely be awhile."

Cecelia followed the direction of his stare and frowned. Aila and Aldridge were skating facing each other. Aldridge had hold of Aila's hands, and it was quite evident that he did not know how to ice-skate. Yet, his deep male laughter and Aila's sweet feminine laughter still filled the air. Despite not knowing what he was doing, Aldridge seemed to be having a grand time just being with Aila. Cecelia started to smile, but then frowned in confusion as she recalled that Aldridge had told her mother that going ice-skating today had been his idea.

"Do you think Lord Aldridge wished to come skating today to learn how?" Cecelia asked Liam.

"Nay," he answered with such surety that Cecelia slowly turned her gaze back to him, curious how he could be so certain.

"Then why did he wish to skate if he does not know how?" she persisted when Liam was not forthcoming with more information.

"He agreed to it at Aila's suggestion so I could have the chance to spend time with ye," Liam said so casually that she almost missed the enormity of his confession. Her heart exploded in her chest as she watched him shake out the blanket he had taken out of the carriage, then let it fall to the ground in a cloud of soft white. When he was done, he faced her, his gaze expectant.

She had to say something, yet she could not say what she truly wished to say—that his words had caused gooseflesh to race across her body and fill her with happiness.

"Tell me about your home," she said instead, sincerely wanting to know but also hoping to avoid any more personal conversation.

Disappointment flashed across his face so quickly that

she would have missed it had she not been staring at him. An easy smile replaced the disappointed look, and he turned from her, grabbed the basket that was filled with food and drink, and held his hand out to her to help her sit down.

She bit her lip, hoping to steel herself against her reaction to him before she took his hand, but it was no use. The moment his fingers curled around hers, she shivered. She did not look at him for fear his eyes would hold the knowledge of how he affected her. Yet when his fingers tightened perceptibly around hers, she had no doubt that he was aware of how he made her feel.

Once she was seated, he released her hand. He removed items from the basket as he spoke. "Dunvegan is my home. I already told ye it's on the Isle of Skye, which is the most beautiful place ye will ever behold in yer life. A loch and craggy rocks surround the castle on one side, and on the other are tall, lush trees and rolling hills. Skye is filled with waterfalls and secret paths and streams, and when ye ride out, whichever way ye look, ye will see animals grazing on green grass and towering, proud peaks beckoning to be climbed." A faraway look swept into his eyes as he spoke of his home. "The air is fresh and the sky a brilliant blue, and ye can just about count on a drizzle of rain every day, which is what makes the land so verra green and glorious, with flowers of purple, yellow, and white. And of course, there is heather that fills the air with the scent of Heaven."

Cecelia could picture Dunvegan in her mind, the wide-open spaces and land untouched by progress the way London had been. "I'd love to see it someday," she said, not realizing how her words would sound until they had left her mouth.

Liam smirked at her, as if he knew she had not meant to say anything that could have been misconstrued, yet he seemed to understand that her enthusiasm at his description had swept her away. He poured a cup of hot chocolate and handed it to her. "Perchance ye will," he said. "Ye never know what the future holds."

"No," she relented, "one never does. But one's future is often shaped by many outside forces that compel choices one might not normally make."

"Possibly," he agreed. "But I'm striving to make choices using both my heart and my head."

She could not help but smile. Liam exuded such raw masculine power, and to hear him speak of his heart made her own heart tug.

"And how has that gone for you in the past? Using both your heart and your head to make decisions?" she asked.

"I'll have to let ye know," he said, grinning slyly. "I've only recently attempted the combination." His voice had dropped to a low, undeniably seductive tone, and his gaze moved slowly from her eyes to her lips.

Her heart pounded so loudly, she was sure he must have heard it. When his focus remained on her mouth, desire ignited. He did not move an inch, yet she felt the caress of his lips on hers as surely as if they had touched. Her breath hitched in her throat. "What are you thinking?" she asked, hoping conversation would cool the longing he created.

His gaze came to her eyes again and impaled her. "I'm thinking," he said, his voice thick, "that if we were alone, I would kiss ye. What do ye think about that?"

She swallowed hard. "I think it's a very good thing we are not alone."

Whatever emotion her answer caused, his cool green eyes did not display. Instead, they narrowed a bit, and determination flared in his gaze. "And why is that, Cecelia?

Do ye not wish for me to kiss ye?"

She should say no. She knew she should. The conversation was improper. *He* had no funds; *she* needed to secure her mother's future to make amends for having a hand in destroying it. This thing, this undeniable attraction, could lead nowhere. Yet, she could not make herself lie.

"I do wish you to kiss me," she whispered. "Truly, I do. But I should not wish it."

"Why should ye not?" he demanded, his emotions now easy enough to recognize as anger tightened his jaw.

Heaven above! She had not wanted to have *this* particular conversation, yet not desiring it would not stop it. Humiliation burned her cheeks. "Liam, I'm not at liberty to do as I wish when it comes to matters of the heart." She felt like a fool blathering on about her heart when they'd only known each other such a short time, yet she had to make it clear that they could be no more than friends.

He said nothing, simply stared at her with unblinking eyes. When she realized he was waiting for her to say more, she cleared her throat. "My father did not leave my mother and myself in the best financial situation." Liam's eyes narrowed a fraction, but she did not blame him for the displeasure they showed. Her words sounded horrid, even to her own ears. "I am somewhat to blame, I daresay, for all that has occurred," she rushed out, wishing the conversation to be over. "And I… Well, you see, my mother needs me to make a good match…if it's possible." Her face burned so hot that she fanned it with her open palm.

He watched her for a moment, his expression guarded yet slightly disappointed, but then suddenly, his face softened. "Tell me, Cecelia. In yer mind, what qualities must a man possess to be a good match worthy of being allowed to court ye?"

"He must be loyal, honorable, witty, and brave," she said without hesitation.

He reached across the distance that separated them and took her hand in his. Even with her gloves on, the heat that radiated from his palm sent delicious shivers through her once more. "I know ye don't know me, but if ye will give me a chance, I hope ye will find that I am all of those things."

The only thing to say was, *No,* he could not have a chance. *They* could not have a chance. But her pulse raced and thoughts spun in her head. "What qualities must a woman you wish to court possess?" she asked in lieu of responding to his confession.

He smiled, looking much like a well-fed cat. "She must be loyal, honorable, witty, and brave."

Her lips parted in shock. "You're teasing me!"

"Never," he said with such vehemence that she believed him. "Never would I tease ye about such a thing. If ye are willing to put yer trust in me, then I will put my trust in ye, and maybe together, we will discover something amazing. Are ye willing?"

She stared into his eyes, so persuasive and tempting, and the wish to say yes danced on her tongue.

"Miss Cartwright!" a voice boomed so near and loud that she jerked. When she looked toward the voice, she could not help but smile at the face of her one-time cohort, Blackmore.

He closed the short distance between them in a few strides, stopped in front of her, and glanced between her and Liam. The moment his gaze fastened on her hand in Liam's, she realized that Liam was still holding it. She quickly tugged it away. She could not afford more talk about her.

Liam arched an eyebrow at her, which made her cheeks burn hotter. She hated to think he might mistakenly believe it was because of his station. It was merely because of her foolish past and her need for a smarter future.

"Cecelia," Blackmore said, abandoning propriety as casually as he had always done. She kept her focus on him, afraid of what Liam must think.

Blackmore's mouth quirked as if he might smile, but then it twisted into a jaded smirk. He had changed in the time he had been gone. His face, once boyishly handsome, had a lean, hard look about it, as if he had seen much that had matured him quickly. His eyes were no longer mischievous but wary, yet still blue as a blindingly bright day. He was still a very handsome man, but he did not compare to Liam. Liam was simply the sort of man who made all others fade into the shadows.

"Is this how you greet an old friend, Cecelia?" Blackmore hitched his eyebrows, and she realized, to her mortification, that she had been staring at him while thinking about Liam.

"Hello, Blackmore," she replied. As she scrambled to get up, her heel caught on the edge of her gown. At once, both men held out a hand to offer her aid. She looked between the men, who were staring at each other with almost identical looks of irritation, and she nearly laughed. Thankfully, she managed to hold it in as she reached out and clasped Liam's hand. He was, after all, sitting by her and, therefore, better positioned to aid her, she told herself. Yet she knew it was a bold lie. She had simply wanted to touch him one more time.

She didn't miss the triumphant look Liam gave Blackmore. Clearing her throat, she waved a hand at Liam. "Your Grace, this is Lord MacLeod."

"Cecelia, I told you years ago to call me Edward," Blackmore said.

She could not help but glance at Liam. What must he be thinking of her?

She took a deep breath. "And I told you then that I couldn't possibly do so." A soft chuckle rumbled from Liam, and she positively knew it was because she had consented to call him by his Christian name in private but had not consented to do so with Blackmore.

Blackmore offered Liam a dark look before smiling gently at her. "As I recall, you also said you could not possibly wade into the water, but with enough persuasion, you did."

She glared at Blackmore for being so inconsiderate as to remind her of that now. "And I paid for that dearly," she replied in a cold voice, the initial feeling of warmth at seeing her old friend starting to fade.

"I have often thought of you," he said, the statement simple yet so very complicated. His voice held undeniable regret.

Her forehead creased as she frowned. What was he doing?

"I don't think Miss Cartwright has thought of ye," Liam said in a voice that chilled her.

She jerked her gaze to him and was shocked to see his pulse ticking furiously at his jaw. Why, he looked livid! Was it because he was jealous? A little thrill shot through her that horrified her at once. She had no right to be happy if he was jealous.

His words of moments before replayed in her mind. He had asked for her trust and a chance to court her. She wanted to let him, but even so, how would she ever convince her mother to agree? Did she even have a right to ask? Wasn't it her duty, after the problems she had caused, to marry as well as she could for her mother's sake?

"Cecelia, did you hear me?" Blackmore asked.

She blinked at him. "No, I'm sorry."

"I was hoping you would allow me to call upon you tomorrow and resume our last discussion."

Her mouth gaped open. He wanted to speak of marrying her? That could not be correct.

He nodded, confirming that he had read her thoughts in her eyes. "Aldridge has told me a bit about your troubles. I know I can help if you will but allow me to. I have longed to do so, you know."

"Come after noon," she rushed out, wishing to make him quit talking. She could hardly believe he might still want to marry her, but if that was what he was trying to tell her, she certainly did not want him to do so in front of Liam.

Blackmore gave Liam a smug look that made Cecelia want to scream. Her heart did not flutter for the man, nor her pulse speed up, nor her thoughts swim, yet if he was offering, she had to accept, didn't she?

He quickly took his leave, and the moment he was gone, she turned slowly to Liam. His face closed immediately but not so fast that she did not see the disappointment. She felt so wretched she wanted to cry.

"Liam, I—"

He pressed a gentle finger to her lips. "Ye do not owe me explanations. I see something in ye, Cecelia, something special."

She had no notion of what to say to those amazing words, but before she could respond at all, Aila and Aldridge appeared. As the two of them partook in the packed food and drink, Cecelia found herself chatting incessantly, trying to fill the silence left by Liam, who sat looking rather distracted and distant. The more she talked, the more apparent she knew it became that something had occurred.

Aila gave her a curious look, and when Liam's sister said they ought to be going, Cecelia had never felt so glad to escape, yet so disheartened to part with someone in her life. She was a confused mess, and it had only taken a few days for the handsome Scot to make her so.

Six

Liam awoke the next morning, determined to get Cecelia alone once more and secure an answer from her about his courting her. The only problem was that he knew her mother would not welcome a visit from him. He was contemplating this problem as he made his way downstairs, when Aila appeared at the bottom of the steps dressed in a riding habit.

He smiled at his sister. "Are ye and Aldridge going riding?"

"We are—along with Miss Cartwright and the Duke of Blackmore."

Liam scowled at the mention of the duke who had spoken to Cecelia in such a personal tone and had gazed at her as if she were a fine whiskey he wished to drink. Liam did not like the man in the least.

Aila gave a soft laugh. "Ye look like ye wish to throttle someone, and I daresay, it is the Duke of Blackmore."

"Ever astute, sister dear," Liam replied.

"Do ye wish to come with us?" Aila asked.

"I most definitely do," he instantly replied.

Riding on her horse in Hyde Park between Blackmore, who

had arrived at her home earlier than she had bid him and who her mother had fairly shoved her out the door to go riding with this morning, and then Liam, who her mother had reminded her would never do, was making Cecelia miserable. She wanted a man whom she could not encourage to pursue her, despite the way his nearness made her stomach flutter, but had to allow the pursuit of a man she did not want.

She simply had to get away from them or she would go mad. As the two men argued among themselves over who was the better rider, Cecelia tried to think of a plausible excuse to leave.

"I know!" Aila exclaimed, making Cecelia's breath catch with a momentary ridiculous thought that the woman had somehow read her mind. But when she turned her attention to Liam's sister, she was looking at Liam and Blackmore, as was Aldridge. No one was paying Cecelia any heed.

"Whichever one of ye wins the race may claim a stroll by the water with Miss Cartwright," Aila said. "I'm sure ye both would agree that is a sufficient prize!"

Cold air hit Cecelia's teeth as her mouth parted in shock. Before she could lodge a protest, both men had agreed and lined up their horses. Now she was not only stuck but she was going to be forced to be alone with either Blackmore or Liam, and she feared the outcome of either instance. What if Blackmore truly did offer for her once more? How could she turn him down when she knew how much it would help her mother? But if Liam won the race, and he perchance kissed her when they were alone, she feared she'd not be able to deny him, and then her heart would most surely be lost to a man she could not possibly have.

As the race started, she pushed her worries to the side

and concentrated on the men. Both were excellent riders. Aila cheered her brother on, and Aldridge stood silent, likely fearing to show favoritism toward either man—one was a longtime friend, and the other his future brother-in-law.

Liam pulled ahead of Blackmore, and a surge of happiness filled her. It was then that Cecelia knew Liam posed the biggest threat to her. Had Blackmore won, she could perchance have managed to turn him from a conversation of marriage, but if Liam tipped her face to his for a kiss, she didn't think she possessed the will to stop him.

Not long later, Liam strode up to her. "Shall we stroll?" he inquired. "Or do you fear being alone with me?" The challenge glinting in his eyes was unmistakable.

She notched up her chin. "Don't be ridiculous," she said archly. "I fear no man."

"Hear! Hear!" Blackmore, who had just walked up, said.

Cecelia glared in his direction, noting Aila's and Aldridge's amused smiles. "Besides," she said, "we are hardly alone in Hyde Park, Lord MacLeod."

"I'll follow behind, if you wish it," Blackmore offered, his hard gaze pinning Liam, then landing on her with questioning eyes.

She should agree. This was the perfect way to avoid giving in to her desires. "There is no need," she said, narrowing her eyes at Liam. "Is there?"

A mischievous smile tugged at his lips. "Not in my mind, Miss Cartwright."

Not a half hour later, after managing to touch on every topic from the weather, to embroidery, to how she had learned to cook and barter, she had to pause to give her poor throat a moment's respite. When she did, Liam grabbed her hand, and her eyes flew first to his face, then scanned around them. With total amazement, she realized they were quite alone on the trail. She had been so preoccupied with keeping control of the conversation and talking continuously so nothing else could occur that she had not even noticed that he had guided her off the main path.

As he turned her purposely to him and tilted up her chin, her heart began to hammer in her chest. "This is not wise," she said, her voice wobbly.

"Because you desire me?"

She nodded, then gasped. "No," she murmured.

Cecelia said one thing aloud, yet her body implied another. Her half-open eyes made him groan. He had not intended to use the walk as an opportunity to get her alone, but he had suddenly found himself here with her. He imagined they had a few short minutes, at best, before Blackmore came looking for her. The duke was no fool, of that Liam was certain, but neither was he. This might be the one chance he would get to learn if she desired him as he hoped, and he was going to take it.

He leaned in and captured her soft lips with his, and when she pressed her body against him and soft mewling sounds came from her, he knew that her craving matched his. As he slanted his mouth over hers, he gathered her into his arms and held her close. She felt so right, as if she fit him perfectly. He traced his tongue over the crease of her lips, and she parted them on a throaty exhalation. When he tasted her sweetness, lust shot through him.

"Cecelia, are you down here?" a voice called like cold water being thrown on them.

With a gasp, she wrenched away from him and scrambled backward, her hands already busily straightening her hair and gown. "Here," she called back, her gaze sweeping around them. "Just admiring the flowers," she added, her voice breathless.

Liam did not stop her from trying to cover the truth of what they had done, but when Blackmore appeared and his keen gaze moved from Liam to Cecelia and back to him with a murderous look, Liam simply smiled pleasantly at the man. Liam had staked his claim, and Blackmore knew it. Now it was up to Cecelia to go with her heart and not her mother's.

Typically, Liam loved to hunt and be outdoors. Yet the day after he shared the kiss with Cecelia, was not one of those days. He found himself in the frustrating position of having to leave for the country for a hunt with Aldridge to which Liam had previously committed. He considered begging off and staying to see Cecelia, but he knew how much it meant to Aila that he and Aldridge become close.

On the first day of the hunt he replayed his kiss with Cecelia a thousand times in his mind. He wished they would have had a chance to speak privately after, but she had immediately claimed she had to return home that day, after Blackmore had found them alone.

By the second day of the hunt, he irritably decided that being such a good brother was a bother. If only he did not love his sister so dearly, he would depart immediately and return to London to see Cecelia.

On the third day of the hunt, he thought of nothing but Cecelia. He was undeniably attracted to her, in both mind and body, but none of that mattered if she chose to follow her mother's wishes. He *could* tell Cecelia the truth of his situation, but he wanted her to choose him without knowing of his wealth and status.

By the end of the week, his frustration vibrated through him, and he knew he could not stay away from London one more day. He glanced around the group of three men and noted a fourth man riding up. Liam turned his attention to Aldridge, dismissing their newest addition for the moment and focusing on the objective of today's hunt. Thus far, Aldridge had chosen said objective every day, and Liam assumed today would be no different. Liam had forced himself to hold back on the entire trip and allowed Aldridge and his friends to pursue the foxes, because if Liam had really employed his hunting skills, he would have tracked and cornered the foxes every day before Aldridge and his friends even managed to crest the first hill toward the woods. It wasn't that the Englishmen were bad hunters, but they had never had to hunt to survive. Liam had, and that taught a man skills that merely hunting for pleasure could never teach.

But his consideration had come to an end. His patience was depleted, and he wanted to find the prey, corner it, and return to London as quickly as possible. "Aldridge, what's our mark for today?"

Aldridge offered an easy smile. "Two red foxes."

Liam nodded. "Once I have them trapped, I'm heading back to London. I'll see ye there, so no need to concern yerself about me."

Aldridge chuckled. "You're awfully certain you will be the one to trap the foxes."

"Aye," Liam agreed, not bothering to soften his tone.

"That may have been the case yesterday, as I was not here," an unfamiliar voice said from behind him.

Liam turned and acknowledged the newcomer. The man was as tall as Liam but not nearly as great in size. His dark eyes reminded Liam of a fox's—clever and calculating. Liam felt an instant distaste for him. The smug look the man gave him and the man's next words firmly sealed Liam's dislike.

"I am the best huntsman in England," the man said, cocksure.

"Only England?" Liam replied, which elicited chuckles from the small group of men.

The man scowled. "You're not English."

"Verra perceptive of ye," Liam responded. "I'm Liam MacLeod, from the Isle of Skye."

A look of disdain crossed the stranger's face. "That explains your boastfulness, but you cannot best me. I'm Viscount Hawkins, and I have been hunting all my life."

"Careful, Hawkins," Aldridge said. "Liam here is the laird of the MacLeod clan, and he has been hunting all his life, as well. He is also my betrothed's brother and my honored guest, so mind the few manners you possess."

Liam sensed that Aldridge did not care for Hawkins, which in Liam's mind made Aldridge an even better man for his sister. But why, then, had Hawkins been invited?

Hawkins's eyes narrowed, but then he seemed to remember himself as a false smile was forced to his lips. "I do apologize, and Aldridge, I appreciate the invitation to hunt."

"Northington here says you are the best hunter he knows, and that piqued my interest," Aldridge replied with a nod at Lord Northington. "Now we shall see."

Aldridge gave Liam a pointed look and understanding dawned. Aldridge wished him to best Hawkins. But how did Aldridge know Liam was capable?

Aldridge stared at Liam as he spoke. "Aila has spoken

often of your hunting skills, and even boldly informed me when I met her that you could teach me a thing or two."

Liam grinned. So Aldridge had suspected Liam had been holding back and wanted to test him? By the smile curling the man's lips, Liam knew the answer.

Within seconds, all the men had mounted their horses. Hawkins maneuvered his horse in front of Liam's and then said over his shoulder, "You may wish to stay back, MacLeod. I'd hate for you to get the dust from my horse's nimble hooves in your eyes."

Liam simply smiled.

When the master of the hounds sounded his horn for the start of the hunt, the foxes were released, and the wildly barking hounds took off, Liam easily moved past Hawkins. He could have left him a great distance behind immediately, but it gave him wicked pleasure to allow the man to ride in his dust for a spell. But when an errant thought of Cecelia entered his mind, he increased his pace, coming closer to the master of the hunt, the rest of the riders far behind them.

They raced through streams, brush, and growth, and jumped several fallen logs to keep up with the hounds in pursuit of the foxes. When Liam looked over his shoulder, only Aldridge and Hawkins remained in sight, and Liam was so far ahead that they'd never catch up.

The master of the hounds waved a hand toward a den where the hounds had circled and were digging the foxes out. He called praise to the pack, followed by promises that the hounds could soon rip the foxes to shreds. But Liam did not wish to see the foxes killed. Unnecessary killing had never given him pleasure. Killing an animal for food or so they would not overpopulate a land was one matter, but to kill simply for sport? That bothered him.

"How does the population of foxes fare here?" he shouted over the hounds' loud barking.

"Scarce currently," the master of the hounds answered.

Suddenly, the foxes darted out, and when the master of the hounds moved to block their escape with his horse and signaled Liam to do the same, Liam let them slip by him.

The master of the hounds gave him a surprised look but did not comment.

Hawkins, who had just ridden upon the scene, bellowed, "Why the devil did you do that?"

Liam narrowed his eyes at the man. "I don't abide killing simply to kill."

Hawkins glared at him. "Perhaps you should have considered that the rest of us wanted to see the foxes killed by the hounds."

"Then ye should practice yer hunting skills so ye can be the first to the hounds. As it is now, ye're fair, at best."

"Do you insult me?"

"Nay," Liam replied, working to bring his temper under control. "I merely state the truth. Now, if ye'll excuse me."

He turned his horse to head back to the house and found Aldridge behind him.

Damnation. He needed to apologize to his sister's betrothed for ruining his hunt. Liam moved his horse close to Aldridge's. When the two men were face-to-face, Liam spoke in a low voice. "I do apologize. I should have made it clear that I don't hunt merely for sport, only out of necessity."

Aldridge smiled and glanced toward the others. "A moment, gentlemen. MacLeod needs to return to London, and I must discuss business with him for a minute."

Liam frowned but followed Aldridge when he turned his horse and walked him a good distance away. As they headed for some trees, they passed the two other men in the party, and Aldridge asked them to wait with Hawkins and the master of the hunt.

Once they were alone, Aldridge gave Liam an amused look. "Aila warned me," he replied, surprising Liam.

"Then ye knew I'd not want to see the foxes killed?"

Aldridge nodded and flicked his gaze to where they had left Hawkins standing. "I don't care for Hawkins, and he'd been bragging at White's about being the best huntsman the day before we were to leave for the hunt. I recalled Aila mentioning your skill and your strict personal rule about only killing animals you intend to eat, and I could not resist the opportunity to see Hawkins bested and angered. I am sorry."

"It's all right," Liam replied with a chuckle. "I enjoyed both, but why do ye not care for Hawkins?"

Aldridge cocked his eyebrow. "Beyond the man's arrogance, I don't believe for a moment that Miss Cartwright, whom I have known since we were children, betrayed him—as he has loudly proclaimed to anyone who will listen—by kissing Lord Tarrymount," Aldridge said in an angry whisper.

Liam's own blood heated at Aldridge's revelation. So *this* was Cecelia's former betrothed…

He glanced over his shoulder at Hawkins and found the man staring in their direction. Liam faced Aldridge once more. "What else can you tell me?" he asked, wishing to have all the facts.

"Unfortunately, my mother and a group of her cronies caught Miss Cartwright with Lord Tarrymount in our library at a party," Aldridge replied.

Liam recalled Cecelia's mention that no one had believed her innocence. He'd heard the heartbreak in her voice, and he knew she had been telling the truth. She had no reason to lie to him. She had not been trying to get him to court her, nor had she even told him what had occurred.

"What happened after they were discovered?" Liam asked.

"I was off at war, but my sister told me that Hawkins immediately broke the betrothal and started courting Miss Cartwright's former best friend within a sennight. They are now betrothed. He apparently made it well known that Miss Cartwright had broken his heart, but I find it odd that a man who claims such a thing would court another woman a mere sennight later, and conveniently the lady he chose to court had a greater dowry than Miss Cartwright's, who I'm sure had a decent one but not a large one. Something just seems false to me, but I cannot deduce exactly what. Perhaps it's simply because I happen to know Hawkins needs to marry a woman with a large dowry, or maybe it's the fact that I don't care for the man." Aldridge shrugged.

Liam's mind turned with all he had just heard. Cecelia and her mother were financially strapped, but apparently that was not known among the *ton*. Perhaps Hawkins had learned of it? He didn't doubt Cecelia would be forthright and honest with her betrothed if her dowry was gone. Had she told Hawkins, and then the man had—

"What sort of lady is Miss Cartwright's former best friend?" he asked.

Aldridge's brows drew together. "An heiress. Shy. Not half as pretty as Miss Cartwright. Very sweet and a tad naive."

"In other words, easily duped?" Liam asked.

"Exactly," Aldridge replied.

"Is it common knowledge in the *ton* that Hawkins is in need of a bride with a large dowry?"

"No," Aldridge replied. "I only recently discovered it upon my return to England when my father brought me into the business of running our estate. Hawkins's father has multiple notes of credit that my father has extended him, which are all past due."

"What do ye think would induce a shy, rather mousy lady, who is a bit naive, to accept an offer from her friend's former betrothed?"

Aldridge rubbed at his jaw for a moment. "I suppose if she had been convinced the man truly had been broken-hearted and that her former friend truly had willingly kissed another man."

Liam nodded. "And it would be so much easier to convince her of that if the lady's friend was made to look like she was a wanton woman…"

Aldridge's mouth parted in obvious shock. "Do you think that Hawkins set Miss Cartwright up to be found in another man's arms?"

"I do. But I'm not sure how to prove it, nor that proving it would make anything better for Miss Cartwright." There was, after all, the secret of her own dire financial situation.

"I wish there were something we could do," Aldridge said.

"Oh, but there is," Liam replied, already turning his horse back to Hawkins.

"What are you doing?" Aldridge bid from behind.

Liam turned in the saddle. "I'm going to give Hawkins a bit of justice. When I give ye the signal, start a conversation about boxing."

"Boxing?" Aldridge repeated, his brow furrowed.

Liam nodded, his blood now rushing through his veins in anticipation.

"What's the signal?" Aldridge asked.

"I'll touch my finger to my nose," Liam hastily replied.

When Liam reached the circle of gentlemen, he announced that he had decided to stay, and then he touched his nose as he purposely met Aldridge's gaze.

"Say," Aldridge said, "I really need to get to Gentleman Jackson's. I've missed the boxing matches we all used to have. Who is the man to beat these days?"

"Hawkins," Aldridge's other guests said in unison.

Liam had to fight the urge not to laugh. He could not have asked for a better lead in to his plan.

"I'm somewhat of a boxer myself," Liam said casually, but with enough of a hint of boastfulness that he felt certain Hawkins would take the bait.

As expected, Hawkins gave a derisive laugh. "When we return to London, we can meet in the ring. I'll show you how a gentleman boxes."

"I see no need to wait until we return to London," he replied, the challenge clear in his words. "We need nothing but our fists and a space within which to box, and we have both right here."

Hawkins's eyebrows shot upward. "We've no gloves."

Liam met the man's surprised gaze and held it. "I've no need of gloves, but if ye're scared, I certainly understand."

Wariness flashed in Hawkins's eyes, but in a breath, Liam surmised that the man was too cocky to decline the challenge. "And what are the stakes?"

"Let us say fifty pounds?"

Liam saw the man flinch, but then Hawkins smirked. "If you wish to be relieved of fifty pounds, I am more than willing to take the funds from you," he replied and moved to dismount his horse.

"And if ye lose?" Liam asked. "Ye do have the funds to pay the bet, don't ye?"

"Of course," Hawkins replied smoothly.

As Liam dismounted his horse, Aldridge caught his gaze, and they exchanged a knowing look. Hawkins was a liar and was about to engage in a bet he was not going to be able to satisfy. Such a man was likely one who would scheme to rid himself of his betrothed, yet ensure he still look like a gentleman in order to capture a new, wealthier bride.

Once both men had taken off their coats, and Hawkins his cravat, they faced each other. "What are the rules?" Hawkins demanded.

Liam offered a grim smile. He'd been fighting barefisted since he was a wee lad. It was somewhat of a sport in his clan. "'Tis simple," he replied. "The first man down is the loser, and payment is due within two days."

Hawkins's lips curled into a mocking smile. "But of course."

"When Aldridge signals, we start," Liam added.

Hawkins nodded, Aldridge gave the signal, and Liam watched, fists raised, as Hawkins began an odd sort of dance. The man shuffled to the left, and then the right, and then back again. He jabbed as he did so, and Liam merely leaned one way, then the other, to avoid the man's punches. But as he did so, he mentally counted beats in his head. Two beats and Hawkins would dance to the left again. One beat and Liam would strike.

Beat.

Liam sent his fist straight at his target. He didn't mind the impact or the sound of crunching bone in the least. He did, however, mind Hawkins's howls of pain. They were rather annoying.

"Do ye want more?" he asked Hawkins as he swayed on his feet.

The man turned rage-filled eyes on Liam. "I'm going to bloody well—"

Whatever Hawkins was "going to bloody well" do, Liam would never know. He shot his fist out to connect nicely with the man's jaw. Hawkins's head jerked backward, and the man stumbled, then crumpled to the ground. He sat on his bottom, blood now gushing from his nose and bottom lip, which Liam realized he must have grazed. He stepped toward Hawkins until he loomed over the man. And then he waited. It took a minute, but Hawkins finally glanced up at him.

"*That* is how a Scot fights," Liam said. He turned on his heel, took his coat from Aldridge, and wasted no time heading back to London.

Seven

"Lord MacLeod," Cecelia's mother said the next afternoon, not bothering to hide her discontent at his arrival at her home, "I'm sorry to inform you that Cecelia is riding in the park with the Duke of Blackmore."

Liam doubted the woman was at all sorry to tell him that, and her next words confirmed it. "Do not bother calling again," she said in a hard tone. "Cecelia has gone riding with His Grace every day for a week."

Damnation. Liam clenched his teeth. Blackmore had no doubt known Liam was with Aldridge in the country, had seen his chance to pursue Cecelia, and had taken it, not that Liam blamed the man.

"What time do ye think she might return?" he asked.

"I hardly know," Lady Thornberry snapped. "But as I said, I think you are wasting your time. As you are not from here and hardly know my daughter, I'm sure you are not aware that Blackmore courted Cecelia very actively before he went off to fight Napoleon. I'm certain he never lost his fondness for her. I'd not doubt if he offered for her today."

Liam wouldn't doubt it, either. What he didn't know was how Cecelia would respond.

"Cecelia is anxiously waiting for this to happen," her mother continued. "She *will* accept him, Lord MacLeod."

Blocking out the doubt that tried to speak in his head,

he nodded to Lady Thornberry. "Thank ye for making everything so clear to me."

For a moment, the lady looked truly sorry, but then it was as if she hardened herself against the emotion. Her shoulders went back, and her chin jutted up. "Good day to you."

"Whatever are ye doing back so soon?" Aila inquired as Liam strode into the drawing room at the Rochburns' home a short time later.

He fell into the chair opposite his sister. "She was not there. Her mother informed me that she was riding in the park with the Duke of Blackmore, as she apparently has done every day since I departed. Lady Thornberry also made sure to tell me that Cecelia would accept an offer of marriage from Blackmore, if one was forthcoming. And the woman was quite certain one would be. It seems Blackmore was courting Cecelia before he went off to fight Napoleon."

"Oh, Liam!" Aila cried. "I am sorry. Why do ye not tell her the truth about yer situation now?"

"Ye know why," he growled.

Aila nibbled on her lip while reaching for her drink, which was sitting on the table. As she did so, she knocked something to the floor. "I almost forgot! A note came for ye!" she exclaimed, reaching for it.

Liam took the note his sister held out to him, broke the seal, and quickly read its contents.

Lord MacLeod,

If you'd be so kind as to call on me at 1:00 p.m. sharp today, I would appreciate it.

All the best,
Elizabeth Burton

He lowered the note and found Aila watching him curiously. "Well?" she demanded, blunt as usual.

"I've an invitation to call upon a dear friend of Cecelia's."

Aila arched her eyebrows. "And will ye?"

"Of course," he said with a wink. "Cecelia might be there."

"Tell me of your ride with the Duke of Blackmore," Elizabeth said to Cecelia.

Cecelia stared into the crackling fire for a moment. "It was pleasant. He's changed a great deal in his time away. He's much more serious now, but in a good way. Yet—" she quirked her mouth in thought "—there are things about him that are the same. He still holds disdain for the *ton* and the rules they demand be followed. And he is still unapologetic for going against the ton's dictates, except he has begged my forgiveness a hundred times for the part he believes he played in my social demise. I told him that I'd made my own choices."

"So you did," Elizabeth said.

A slight sharpness in her tone drew Cecelia's attention to her friend. "Are you cross with me?"

"No, my dear! I am worried about you. I see what is happening. You are allowing your mother's wishes to dictate the choices you make. You don't brighten at all when you speak of Blackmore, but the one time you spoke of Lord MacLeod, you positively glowed."

Despair filled Cecelia. Liam had made her feel things she had never felt—strange, wonderful things. She had been unable to put him out of her mind, despite trying, but he had apparently had no problem putting her out of his mind. He'd not come to see her since they had shared their kiss. She told herself it was for the best, but that did not make it hurt less.

She felt Elizabeth's stare on her. "You know my situation," Cecelia said. "If I had acted like a proper lady, I would not be where I am today." Her throat ached to finally speak the truth of her heart. "Perhaps Papa would still be alive if I had been married before his ruination and he'd not had the worry of me on top of everything else."

"You cannot blame yourself for your father's death."

Cecelia sighed. "Can I not?" She was not entirely certain.

Elizabeth shook her head.

Cecelia gave a faint smile. "I have no dowry, and Mama does not have enough funds on which to live comfortably. What choice do I have but to marry well?"

When Elizabeth simply stared at her, as if she thought there were, indeed, another choice, Cecelia became frustrated. "If Lord MacLeod did have a tendre for me—which his lack of attempt to see me shows he does *not*—how could we possibly make a go of it? He said himself that his clan has seen hard times, just as the others."

Elizabeth scowled. "You need luxury, then, to love a man?"

"Heavens, no!" Cecelia exclaimed. "All I truly want is love, but what of my mother?"

"She could come live with you, if you ended up wedding Lord MacLeod. He looked quite capable of caring for you and many others. I sincerely doubt 'hard times' means you would not have food or a roof over your head."

Cecelia contemplated Elizabeth's words as the memory of Liam's lips on hers stirred her blood. She feared her heart had been lost to him the moment his lips met hers, perhaps even before when he had bought her the book of poetry.

"Mama would never consent to go live in Scotland," she murmured, not wanting to hope yet it sprung within her as she replayed the kiss. She was only human, after all, and the heart wanted what it wanted, despite the utter foolishness of it. Liam *had* desired her. Perhaps he had not come around because he feared she would deny him. But if she saw him and encouraged him...

"If your mother refused to go, that would be her choice. You must make yours, for you are the one who has to live with the decision forever. If it were me, having to part with the trappings of luxury would not compare to having to part with the man I loved, and if your mother truly loves you and wants to see you happy, she will think the same."

Elizabeth's words struck like a stake to Cecelia's heart. She realized that she agreed completely with her friend, yet she knew well how her mother felt about Liam. She'd made it clear when Cecelia had mentioned that perhaps he might court her.

Cecelia once again stared into the fire as she considered everything. She knew her mother loved her, and that her mother was scared for both their futures so was doing what she thought was best.

"My lady," Cooper said, snapping Cecelia's thoughts away from her troubles and to the butler.

"Yes?" Elizabeth replied.

"Lord MacLeod is here to see you."

"Then, by all means, show him in to the drawing room, Cooper."

As Cooper nodded, then hurried to do Elizabeth's bidding, hopeful expectation burst within Cecelia. But nervousness swiftly followed. She turned to Elizabeth. "Did you invite Lord MacLeod here?"

"I did," Elizabeth replied, matter-of-fact.

Cecelia swallowed hard, trying to stifle the worry that he'd be irritated when he realized she was here. "What if he does not care to see me?"

"Don't be ridiculous, my dear. Any man with two good eyes would wish to see you."

Before Cecelia could reply, Liam was suddenly there, consuming the doorway. Cecelia gulped at the sight of him. He was even more beautiful and more virile than she had remembered. He wore tan breeches that appeared to be made of soft leather that molded to his legs like a second skin and made her belly tingle. His white cambric shirt was open at the collar where most Englishmen would have had it closed and worn a cravat, he did not. Liam's skin showed all the way down to the top of his chest. As he and Elizabeth exchanged polite greetings, Cecelia ran her gaze over him, soaking up every glorious detail.

Suddenly, Elizabeth stood to leave, making an excuse that she needed to get something from her bedchamber. She parted in a swish of skirts, and then Cecelia found herself utterly alone with Liam.

"Hello, Cecelia," he said, his voice rich, deep, and music to her ears.

"Hello, Liam," she returned, wincing at her breathlessness.

"May I sit?" he asked, motioning to the space beside her on the settee.

As he did so, she noticed his hand was cut on his knuckles. "What happened to your hand?" she asked, bringing her eyes to his face.

He did not respond at first but strode across the room and sat next to her, so close that their legs pressed against each other's. Blood surged from every part of her body to the places where they touched.

He turned the full force of his gaze on her, not bothering to hide the fact that he was staring at her. "I had to teach a cocky Englishman a lesson," he replied, giving her such a galvanizing look that a tremor coursed through her.

She barely resisted the urge to fan herself. "Who was the man?"

Liam shifted his body to turn more toward her, and his knee bumped hers. She said a silent prayer that he would not move it, and when he didn't, she could barely control her smile. A smile tugged at his mouth, as well. "A verra annoying fellow by the name of Lord Hawkins."

Cecelia gulped.

"Do ye know him?" Liam asked, studying her.

His eyes held a knowing look that made her sure he already knew the answer to that question. "Yes," she said, not bothering to disguise her disdain. "We were betrothed for a short time, but he broke it off."

"Ye must tell me some time why he would do such a thing. He's surely a fool."

Liam's words made her heart squeeze.

"He is a fool, indeed," she managed, and then blurted, "Where have you been?"

"Do ye care?" he asked with quiet intensity.

Her heart thundered almost painfully. Now was the time for a choice as Elizabeth had said: choose the possibility of love, or the possibility of a marriage of comfort. She wanted to grasp at the hope of love, and maybe, just maybe, it would be hers.

"Yes," she whispered. "I care. Very much."

He reached out and ran a lone finger up her arm, trailing gooseflesh everywhere he touched. "I thought ye might not, as I heard ye have been riding in the park with the Duke of Blackmore every day."

"Who told you that?" she asked, surprised that someone would speak of her to Liam at all.

He smiled. "Yer mother. I went to call on ye earlier when I returned to Town—"

"You were away from London?" She gasped. "I thought mayhap—Well, I thought that—"

She simply could not say it.

His hand suddenly came to her cheek, his touch like a hot brand upon her skin. "Ye thought ye had scared me off?"

How was it he could always read her thoughts? She didn't know, but she adored it.

She nodded.

"I can assure ye, Cecelia, I don't scare easily."

His eyes held so much passion and tenderness that she had to curl her toes on a wave of desire and contentment.

"Have ye made a choice, then, between me and Blackmore?" he asked point-blank.

"I didn't realize I had a choice to make," she said, trying to make light of the conversation, which was rapidly growing serious.

"Ye know verra well that ye do," he replied, his tone not amused at all.

She sobered instantly. Fear was making her behave unlike herself, like a scared mouse. She wanted to be a lioness. "I think of him as a friend," she stated firmly.

"Does he know that?" Liam asked gently.

"Well, I have not come out and bluntly said it, but I

have avoided anything that might lead him to think otherwise."

Liam's eyes narrowed and took on lethal glint. "Like a kiss?"

"The only kiss I have shared, as of late, has been with you," she replied, completely breathless. She felt drugged by his closeness. As he leaned toward her, she closed her eyes, wishing with all her heart that he would kiss her once more.

"Here we are!" Elizabeth boomed.

Cecelia shot away from Liam as if he were on fire. He, on the other hand, casually draped his arm along the back of the settee. "What have ye there, Lady Burton?" he asked.

Elizabeth offered him a knowing smile that made Cecelia giggle. "Here," she said, holding up a sloshing bowl, "I've raisins soaked in brandy. This was always a Christmastide game we played in my home. My husband and I used to do it, but I've not done it since his death. I thought maybe…perhaps the two of you would play the game with me?"

"How do we play?" Cecelia asked, rising as one with Liam.

Elizabeth gave them a sly grin. "We blow out the candles, light the brandy, and try to grasp a raisin and eat it without getting burned."

"But that's very dangerous!" Cecelia exclaimed.

"Everything worth doing in life has risk, Cecelia," Elizabeth replied, and Cecelia knew in that moment that her friend was referring to Liam, not the game.

"All right." She nodded. "I'll attempt it if Liam will." She gave him a challenging look.

He winked at her. "I cannot verra well let a lady make me look scared."

Soon the candles were all blown out, the brandy lit, and

each of them took a turn trying to grasp a raisin. Liam was the only successful player, and after much laughter, they quit the game and settled in front of the fire with cups of hot chocolate while Liam regaled them with stories of his childhood and his family.

With every word he spoke, her certainty that she had unwittingly given her heart to him grew.

Elizabeth nudged Cecelia. "The sky is growing dark. Won't your mother be expecting you?"

"Yes, but she thinks I'm still riding in the park with Blackmore. I had him bring me here, instead of home. She won't fuss so about my lateness since she thinks I'm with him."

Foolishly, she had not thought about how her words might make Liam feel, until she glanced at him and saw a pinched look on his face. Biting her lip, she rose and prayed he might offer to walk her home. When he did, she nearly sagged with relief.

Once they were outside, it struck her that she did not even know why he had fought with Jonathan. As they strolled toward her home, she glanced at Liam. "Why did you fight with Lord Hawkins?"

"Because," Liam replied, his voice hard, "Aldridge told me that Hawkins needed to marry for money, and I deduced that ye likely told him of yer father leaving ye and yer mother with scarce funds. From there, it was a short leap to the obvious fact that the blackguard had devised a way to exit yer betrothal yet be looked upon as the victim and, therefore, make it likely to catch an unsuspecting, rather naive lady as his next victim—yer friend, Lady Matilda."

She looked at him, wide-eyed. "I suspect the same thing! What I have never understood was why Lord Tarrymount would do that to me..."

Liam's eyes narrowed. "I don't know, either, but I vow to find out and make the man pay."

Cecelia paused in front of her home. "You would do that for me?" she asked, amazed.

He reached out, grasped her hand in his, and very slowly pulled off each finger of her glove. Then he brushed a delicate kiss to the tip of each of her fingers. She was trembling all over by the time his eyes, burning with desire, met hers.

"Ye have bewitched me, Cecelia. I would do anything for ye. And I have something I need to tell ye," he said, his fingers curling tightly around her hand.

The front door of her home burst open then, and her mother stormed out. "Cecelia, go inside," she said in a steely tone.

Her mother was much harder to deny when pitiful than when she acted like this mean person Cecelia hardly recognized. Anger stirred in her breast, and she squeezed Liam's hand.

"No, Mama. I love Liam," she blurted, hearing his sharp intake of breath at her words.

"Oh, Cecelia! You stupid, foolish girl," her mother cried. "Love hardly matters! I have, just an hour ago, accepted a marriage offer from Blackmore on your behalf. You are betrothed, except for the technicality of formally accepting him yourself."

Cecelia shook her head. "I cannot do that, Mama. I'm sorry."

"You would willfully ruin me and yourself?" her mother

moaned to Cecelia.

"Ye won't be ruined, Lady Thornberry," Liam assured her, wishing he'd had the chance to tell Cecelia the truth of his affairs in private first. But her profession of love still rang in his ears, and his chest squeezed mercilessly. He loved her, as well, and he feared suddenly that by holding the truth from her, he had risked losing her. Yet, surely, she would understand why he had done it, he told himself.

"Of course we will be ruined if the two of you were to marry! Laughingstocks and all poor as church mice!"

"Nay." He shook his head. "I'm quite well-off. I'm laird of my clan, and it is very stable. My father sold a large tract of land before he died, and it enabled our clan to prosper once more with smart decisions and hard work."

Cecelia pulled her hand from his as her mother gasped and exclaimed her pleasure. "Oh, Lord MacLeod! I simply knew it! I can explain my behavior."

He ignored her and turned to Cecelia, who had stepped away from him. Tears sprang to her eyes.

"You lied to me," she whispered.

"I wanted to ensure ye wanted me for simply myself." He cringed at how idiotic his reasoning now sounded.

"You *lied* to me," she repeated, her tortured voice searing his soul with pain. "Could you not see that I was not the sort of lady who would marry just for convenience?"

"I—" The words froze on his tongue. "I can now," he said lamely.

She pressed her cheeks to her hands. "I'm a fool," she said, her voice cracking. "I thought we had fallen in love. You made me believe it was possible to have fallen so fast, so completely. I thought I knew you!" She whirled away from him, but he caught her by the arm and turned her back.

He could not let her go. He could not imagine life without her. "Cecelia." He pressed his lips close to her ear and felt her grow tense under his touch. "Ye do know me. The money does not change who I am."

"If you truly believed that," she said in flat tone, "you would have told me. Please, let me go."

"Cecelia, I love ye. I wish to marry ye," he admitted, not giving a damn that her mother stood on the steps, open-mouthed and staring at them.

"Marry me? You do not even know me, and despite what you say, it is now clear to me that *I* don't know *you*! I thought you honest. You told me it was customary where you lived to speak the truth, and I believed you, yet you lied to me! I was truthful with you, told you I was not free to marry as I pleased. You must have seen my torment, seen how I was struggling to accept what I thought I must do to help my mother after meeting you, yet you stayed silent."

The words sounded torn from her throat, and it nearly killed him to hear it. As she fled up the steps without looking back, he felt as if he was losing a part of himself he had only just found.

Cecelia flung the front door open and slammed it shut behind her, leaving him standing in the snow and staring up at her mother, who stood still gawking.

A long silent moment passed before Lady Thornberry spoke. "She will come around. You'll see."

He did not even care that Lady Thornberry only now desired him for Cecelia because of his money. He only cared about getting Cecelia back, but he feared he had been the biggest sort of fool and that she would never trust him again.

Eight

Several days later, on Christmas Eve, as Cecelia sat listless on the settee and watched her mother enter and exit the drawing room, her face first looking enraged and then stupefied, Cecelia wondered just how much worse she could feel.

"Two marriage proposals," her mother wailed. "One from a duke and one from a laird of a Highland clan, and you have rejected them both! I don't imagine we will have anything to eat tomorrow for a Christmastide feast," her mother said shrilly. "We have no funds left to buy any food! We are nearly beggars!"

Cecelia rose on shaky legs with a heart that had been shattered and went to her room, where she had hidden money she had made some months ago by selling her few pieces of jewelry. She gathered the money, marched downstairs with it, and plunked it on the table before her mother. "This will give us some time. I will secure a job as a seamstress, a cook, or perhaps a maid within a sennight. I vow it."

Her mother's answer was the loudest wail Cecelia had ever heard from her. It was so loud that Cecelia nearly missed the knock at the door. As they had been forced to let the butler go the day before, Cecelia made her way to the entrance, and when she opened it, she blinked at the sight of

Cooper. Her first thought was that something had happened to Elizabeth.

"What's the matter?" she cried, no longer caring that her mother would learn of her friendship with Elizabeth. Cecelia would be friends with whomever she chose from this moment forward.

Cooper held out what appeared to be an invitation. Frowning, Cecelia took it, opened it, and read it.

Dearest Cecelia,

I would so love if you and your mother might join me for a Christmastide feast tomorrow, if you think you can convince your mother to darken my door.

All the best,
Elizabeth

Cecelia folded the paper and glanced over her shoulder at her mother, who had come up behind her and clearly had read the note over Cecelia's shoulder.

"Certainly not," her mother snapped.

Cecelia ignored her, and it felt heavenly. "Tell Elizabeth that I shall be there," she told Cooper.

The butler grinned. "I'll convey the good news," he said, then turned to go.

Cecelia closed the door and faced her mother. "I *am* going."

"I'll not go with you," her mother said, giving Cecelia a wounded look that made her lose her last bit of control.

"Mama, I am the heartbroken one! The wounded one. I am sorry I failed you! I'm sorry for my fault in Papa's death! But I cannot marry Blackmore. I don't love him! And I cannot marry Lord MacLeod, as he clearly does not truly love me!"

"Oh, Cecelia!" her mother cried, a horrified look coming over her face. "You are not at all to blame for your father's death, and I—" She had to pause because, to Cecelia's amazement, she choked up. "I simply wanted to spare you the hardships I endured by being poor. I've failed you!" her mother lamented and burst into tears.

A trace of amusement filled Cecelia as she moved to soothe her mother. Leave it to Mother to need mollifying when Cecelia was the injured party. Yet, somehow, hovering over her mother, quieting her tears, and whispering words of reassurance made Cecelia feel stronger, as if they would, indeed, survive whatever came to them.

After a bit, her mother suddenly stopped crying, and she wiped her face and squared her shoulders as a look of fierce determination spread across her face. Cecelia didn't know what to make of the transformation, nor what to think when her mother gripped her by the shoulder and stared into her eyes. "Cecelia, I may have failed you before now, but I will not fail you any longer."

"Mother—"

"No," her mother interrupted, "you must allow me to speak. What I say might make you cross with me all over again, but I must say it. Come sit with me," she commanded, yet her voice was gentle. Once they were settled on the settee, her mother shocked her by sliding an arm around Cecelia's shoulder and stroking her hair. "Darling, I believe you have been too harsh with Lord MacLeod."

Cecelia stiffened. She was sure her mother was now Liam's biggest advocate because she knew he was well-off.

Her mother looked suddenly sad as she squeezed Cecelia's shoulder. "I see the look on your face," she whispered in a shamed tone, "and I can understand it. If I were you, I would also believe I was only saying this because I now know he can take care of you. I'm not going to lie—it greatly pleases me to know that he has the means to ensure you will never have to know a day of hunger or fear you may not have a roof over your head, but what pleases me more than this is that I truly believe he loves you."

"But he lied to me," Cecelia replied. "He didn't know me well enough to be certain that I would not marry him simply for his money."

Her mother frowned at her. "Of course he didn't know of your wonderful character, Cecelia. He had to learn it first. And, after all," Mother said in a chiding tone, "you said yourself that you made it clear to him from the beginning that you needed to make a marriage of convenience. Put yourself in his place. What if you were the heiress and he was a man without funds who told you from the start that he needed to wed a lady of means? What would you do? Would you immediately have put your faith in a man you had only just met but had an instant liking for, or would you decide to see if a true affection grew and then tell him the truth of it?"

She bit her lip, thinking, but it only took a moment to know what was in her heart. She would have done exactly as Liam had! She swallowed the despair in her throat. "What have I done?" she moaned. "I've ruined everything, I'm certain."

"Shh. Don't give up hope so easily," her mother cooed. "Oh! I know!" she cried. "It is not yet too late to go call on his sister, and when we do, hopefully, he will be there and the two of you can talk!"

Cecelia's heart leaped with hope even as her stomach knotted with fear of rejection. She scrambled to her feet, refusing to allow the fear to stop her from trying to smooth things over with Liam.

Half an hour later, she stood, clutching her mother, in the shadow of a tree they had scrambled behind. Cecelia fought the desire to cry as she stared across the street at Liam, who was entering the Rochburns' home with Francis Dentington on his arm. She could not see Liam's face, but Francis was smiling up at him with a look of devotion that could not be mistaken.

Heaviness pressed on Cecelia's chest. He had already turned his attention to another.

"Cecelia?" her mother asked with care.

Cecelia shook her head, watching as Liam disappeared through the Rochburns' front door. "Let us go home," she said, struggling not to cry. She did not wish to come apart in front of her mother.

"Perhaps it's not as it appears," her mother offered.

Cecelia nodded. "Perhaps," she agreed, but only so her mother would not say more. Cecelia felt raw, and if she tried to discuss Liam, the thread that was holding her together would unravel. So instead of waiting for her mother to say more, Cecelia rushed back toward their house and straight for her room.

On Christmas Day, Cecelia and her mother made their way to Elizabeth's home for the Christmastide feast. Cecelia was surprised at her mother's willingness—no, true eagerness—to go. Mother had been to the market early that morning—also to Cecelia's shock—and she had only come back home to fetch Cecelia just as it was time to leave. Her mother had been in a peculiarly good mood, but Cecelia was horribly gloomy, which struck her as an ironic change of positions.

When they entered Elizabeth's festive home, Cecelia

watched in amazement as her mother's good mood became festive, as well, and her face actually lit up and glowed with delight. Her mother and Elizabeth huddled on the settee exchanging stories of Christmastides past, while Cecelia sat near the fire alone. She forced a smile every now and then when they glanced her way, but she felt as if a dark shroud permanently covered her heart.

Her thoughts drifted to Liam as she turned and stared into the bright flickering flames. She could not help but wonder what he was doing today. Was he with Francis perhaps?

Moments later, when Cooper announced the arrival of Aila, Aldridge, and Blackmore, Cecelia's heart ached with sadness that Liam must either be with Francis or simply had not wanted to be wherever Cecelia was.

She scrambled to her feet, frowning when she realized her mother did not look at all surprised to see the trio. But her attention was diverted when Blackmore took off his hat and Cecelia realized both his eyes were blackened.

"Whatever happened to your eyes?" she exclaimed, rushing to him.

Blackmore gingerly touched the purpled skin with a wince. He gave her a rueful look. "MacLeod challenged me to a boxing match at Gentleman Jackson's over you, and the result was this." He pointed to his face.

"But that's wonderful!" she exclaimed, hope coming to her heart once more.

Blackmore looked at her oddly. "You think it wonderful that I have been wounded?"

His offended tone made her chuckle. "No!" she assured him.

He nodded. "Good. The victor won the prize of getting to come here today to see you. We agreed it would be awkward for both of us to try to win your affection at the same time."

"You don't mean to tell me you won?" she blurted.

Blackmore scowled at her. "No," he replied glumly.

"I knew it could not be so!" she exclaimed.

Blackmore's scowl deepened. "Your lack of confidence in me is rather off-putting, Miss Cartwright," Blackmore grumbled.

"I am sorry, Blackmore," she hastened to apologize for wounding his pride. Then thinking upon his sudden formality with her she added, *"Miss Cartwright?"*

"Indeed. MacLeod threatened to repeat our match if I dared to call you Cecelia ever again."

"This is splendid!" Cecelia exclaimed.

"I'm glad I can bring you cheer," Blackmore said dryly.

Cecelia frowned with sudden worry. "If Lord MacLeod won the match, then why are you here? Not that I am not glad to see you. You are my dear friend."

"Yes, yes," Blackmore said, waving a hand at her. "MacLeod acquired an engagement for a duel right after beating me soundly, so I decided to take advantage of my good fortune and come try to win your affection, which I now see is an utter waste of time."

"I am sorry," she said, feeling guilty. Yet she knew Blackmore did not truly love her, so he would be quite all right. Her pulse had ticked up several beats, and she found she was wringing her hands as she thought about what Blackmore had said of Liam. "Whatever do you mean he acquired an engagement for a duel?"

Aldridge answered her question in an oddly cheerful tone. "Lord Tarrymount happened into Gentleman Jackson's after MacLeod trounced Blackmore."

"Let's not say he *trounced* me," Blackmore said, sulking.

Aldridge shrugged. "After MacLeod used Highland trickery to connect his fists repeatedly to Blackmore's face—"

Blackmore nodded. "Much better."

Aldridge smirked at his friend. "MacLeod challenged Lord Tarrymount to meet him either in the ring or on the field of honor for his part in ruining your good name."

Cecelia clamped her mouth shut when she felt her jaw fall open. "And Lord Tarrymount chose to duel?"

"I would have done the same," Aldridge said. "At the time of the challenge, we all thought Blackmore quite dead from the force of MacLeod's hits."

"I did not even swoon," Blackmore growled.

"No, indeed," Aldridge rushed to agree, though he gave both Aila and Cecelia an amused look. "You were simply resting, unresponsive, with your eyes closed."

"Quite right!" Blackmore thundered.

"Where is this duel?" Cecelia demanded. She simply had to stop it. She'd never be able to live with herself if Liam died defending her honor.

"I'll take you," Aldridge offered. "You'll never find the glade on your own."

Cecelia glanced at Aila, who stood there calmly. "Why are you here?" She knew her voice was near a screech, but she did not care. "Are you not worried for your brother's life?"

"Certainly not," Aila responded confidently. "They are using rapiers, and whoever draws first blood is the victor. Liam will win."

Cecelia wanted to throttle Liam's sister. "And if Lord Tarrymount manages to strike a blow and your brother gets an infection and dies? This is madness! Who is his second?"

"Our younger brother Alistair. He only just arrived in

Town," Aila said.

Cecelia was so upset, she wanted to scream at Aila for not talking Liam out of the duel. Instead, she turned to her mother. "Mama, I must go!"

"I'll go with you," her mother replied. "I have grown quite fond of Lord MacLeod."

Cecelia was struck speechless for a moment. When the ability to speak finally returned, she demanded, "Exactly when did you have the opportunity to grow fond of him? I know you said you understood why he did what he did, but now you say you have grown fond of him, too? When?"

"This morning," her mother said primly. "He sent me a note begging me to meet him at the Rochburns' home. Of course, I did not refuse, as I know how you truly feel about him."

Cecelia did not feel the slightest embarrassment at her mother's pronouncement. "What did he want?"

"Why, he wished for me to tell him every single detail I could recall about you. He said he wanted to show you that he knew you and loved you."

Cecelia was about to ask her mother if Liam had mentioned Francis when Elizabeth spoke. "He came to me yesterday asking questions about you, too," she offered.

"And me, last night," Aldridge said.

"And me, after he blackened my eyes," Blackmore supplied.

Cecelia's heart nearly burst with happiness. He loved her. It didn't matter why Francis had been on his arm yesterday. Cecelia believed with all her heart that he loved her. She had been the biggest sort of fool for ever getting so angry with him.

A few moments later, she sat squashed in a carriage between her mother and Aila as they raced, on Cecelia's command, toward the dueling green.

Cecelia took her mother's hand in hers. "Did you tell Liam—"

Her mother gasped at Cecelia's use of Liam's proper name.

Cecelia just grinned. "Did you tell him how terribly I feel for being so cross and ridiculous and how I went to see him?"

Her mother shook her head. "I thought perhaps it might be best coming from you. I know, if it were me, I would want to hear such wonderful news from the lips of the lady who had my heart and not her mother, who had been so horrid. I did tell him not to give up hope, though."

The heaviness in her chest lifted as she leaned over and kissed her mother's cheek. Not only had Liam given her love but he had given her mother—the wonderful, caring, thoughtful lady she had once been—back to Cecelia.

Defeating Tarrymount in the duel was not satisfying in the least. Perhaps because the man had cried like a wee babe the entire time and blubbered that Hawkins had threatened to expose Tarrymount's own gambling debts if he had not helped Hawkins besmirch Cecelia's name, but more likely it was because Liam feared nothing would bring Cecelia back to him. He felt nothing but darkness. Despite Cecelia's mother telling him not to give up hope, he worried his withholding the truth from her was an unforgivable breach of her trust.

As Tarrymount climbed into his carriage with the aid of Hawkins—who had been too afraid to get out of the carriage, though he was supposed to be Tarrymount's second—Liam bent down and wiped his blade against the grass to clean it. Immediately after the duel was over, he had sent Alistair away, when his younger brother had told him that he should just forget Cecelia, so when Liam heard carriage wheels turn behind him, he assumed Tarrymount and Hawkins were now departing.

Liam squatted there and thought upon if he should go to Lady Burton's home today. Perhaps it was too soon. He did not want to push Cecelia further away, but he missed her with an ache that throbbed in his chest. As a bird call filled the silent glade, Liam squeezed his eyes shut and imagined Cecelia standing there in front of him. He thought about what he would say to her if she were here.

"I'm a fool," he said aloud. "I listened to my head when I should have heeded my heart. I love ye. I love ye, and I cannot imagine life without ye. I want to wrap ye in my arms and carry ye away to my home where I will keep ye hidden away in our bedchamber, worshipping yer body until I know every curve, every dip, every gentle swell of ye by heart."

"Oh, that sounds perfectly wonderful," a soft voice said.

Liam's eyes flew open, and he glanced up at Cecelia, who was standing not a few steps from him. The sun shone down upon her, almost drawing a bright halo over her head.

As he stood, his heart thundered. "Cecelia, I am verra sorry."

She rushed to him and wrapped her arms about his neck. It was all the invitation he needed. He held her tightly to him and buried his face in her fragrant hair. "I love ye, I love ye. I was a fool. Please say ye will marry me."

"Yes!" she exclaimed. She pressed her mouth to his to claim a kiss as only his bold, bonny future bride would dare to do. He took advantage of the moment to show her, through his kiss, the hold she had upon his heart. When they parted, he felt smugly confident that he had succeeded by her lovely, disheveled state. Her rosy, swollen lips and slumberous eyes made him quite happy.

She raised her hand to his cheek and cupped it. "I came to see you yesterday to tell you what a fool I had been, but I saw you entering the Rochburns' home with Miss Dentington on your arm, so I fled."

His chest squeezed mercilessly that she had been caused more pain by such an innocent thing. Francis had caught him unaware as he had been going up the steps to the townhome, and she had slipped her arm in his. "Cecelia, I assure ye—"

She pressed her finger to his lips. "There is no need to assure me of your love. I know it's mine, Liam, and I have never had a greater treasure in all my life. I will never doubt you again."

"Nor I ye," he vowed and sealed it with a kiss that left them both gasping.

Cecelia splayed her fingers over his heart. "Now that," she said with a devilish grin, "is a kiss worth having one's reputation destroyed."

Epilogue

One year later
Dunvegan Castle
Christmas Day

"Darling," Cecelia murmured as Liam showered delicious kisses over her belly, now swollen with child, and all the way up to her neck. He nuzzled her there and then moved onward to her lips, which he claimed in a passionate kiss that made her toes curl and stole her good sense. They really must get out of bed, get dressed, and go to the great hall to celebrate Christmastide with their guests. Her mother would be terribly cross that they were holding up the festivities, and it really was quite rude to keep Aila, Elizabeth, Aldridge, and Blackmore waiting. They had, after all, graciously traveled from London to Skye to spend Christmastide with them.

Yet as Liam lavished her with slow, drugging kisses, her body came alive with the need to respond. Her husband, knowing her so very well, gave her all that she needed and more, so that it was not until much later that she could think past anything other than how he made her skin tingle, breath catch, and heart flutter, and how he gave her such happiness that she thought she would burst.

As he threaded his fingers through her hair, she knew there was something she was forgetting, but she could not remember what. When her stomach growled, she gasped and immediately sat up. "You devil!" she exclaimed playfully. "You knew you would make me forget the festivities, but you cannot make me forget the feast!" She giggled. "Everyone must be starving!"

"Nay," he said, plating a kiss first on her forehead, then her nose, and finally her lips. He grinned at her as he stood, strode to the table in the far corner of the room, and came back holding the book of poetry he had purchased for her the previous year. "I told them to start without us. I wanted to read to the wee babe before we went down as ye said he's been kicking a lot of late. And I knew ye would not take the time for yerself if I was not verra persuasive."

"You know I cannot argue with such a sweet gesture," she replied, taking the kiss he gave her as he sat beside her.

He put his hand on her belly and read a bit of Byron aloud. As he did so, the baby kicked as if to say he heard Liam, and then settled down and was still.

She smiled at her husband. "How did you know it would calm him?"

"He's yer son, aye? Poetry calms ye, so I assumed it would him, as well."

"You know me so well, my love," she replied, brimming with happiness. It was the simple truth, and it was all she needed.

Dear Readers,

I invite you to try When a Highlander Loses His Heart (Highlander Vows: Entangled Hearts Book 4)

One

1359
Loch Awe, Scotland

A chapel was supposed to be a place of sanctuary for Isobel Campbell, but she had a bad feeling that something was very wrong. At first glance, Innis Chonnell Castle, her father's home, had appeared inviting. She had never lived there before, but with the crackling fire, fresh rushes underfoot, bright tapestries hanging on the walls, and warm glow cast over the tiny room, the chapel seemed like a haven. It was contrary in nearly every way from the cold, drab nunnery she'd grown up in, except one—both places were filled with liars. She was as sure of that fact as she was that a storm was coming.

Dampness clung to the heavy air, and it pressed on her like a thick cloak. The sweet pungency of the coming rain filled her nose with every inhalation, and her skin tingled from a strange current in the air. She knew the signs of a storm brewing because her father had taught them to her during one of his yearly birthday visits. He had left her in the protection of the sisters at Iona Nunnery when she was barely a week old, but he never missed her birthday.

Deceitful people were harder to recognize than an impending storm, of course, but in her years living with the nuns, she'd learned that if you spent enough time around people who were attempting to mislead you, eventually they would forget to put their masks on. Only then could you see the ugly truth they'd been striving to hide. It could take a great deal of time, though. Sometimes years, as it had with Sister Beatrice.

Isobel rubbed her fingers over the rough scars on her knuckles. Every time Sister Beatrice had thrashed her until her hands were bleeding, the woman had claimed that she punished Isobel because she loved her. Isobel clenched her teeth with the memory of the lie. The nun had loved the power the punishment had given her, and that was all.

Isobel stole a quick glance at the corner of the chapel where Jean, her stepmother—whom she had only met mere hours earlier—stood with a priest. Jean caught Isobel's gaze and glared at her with hostile eyes.

"What are ye gaping at?" Jean snarled.

A liar, Isobel thought, but she simply pressed her lips together and shook her head. Jean snorted in disgust, then resumed her frenzied whispering to the priest. Unease danced along Isobel's skin, along with the certainty that there was no time to peel back the disguises of the strangers surrounding her.

Many times had she imagined the day she would reach eighteen summers. Those dreams had nothing to do with the fact that she would then be the heiress of Brigid Castle and everything to do with the fact that when she turned eighteen her father would finally take her home with him instead of leaving her at Iona as he did after every other visit. She cared naught for the power Brigid brought her as key to the Scottish Isles; she cared only to be with her father and her half brothers, Findlay and Colin.

When she had dreamed of her eighteenth birthday, her father and brothers came to the nunnery as they always did, and such happiness filled her to see those she loved so dearly. But her dream differed from reality in that when they departed at the end of the day on her eighteenth birthday, she was not left standing alone watching them ride off together, her chest aching with loneliness and longing to go with them. But her dream had not come true as she had thought it would. While she *had* left Iona Nunnery on her eighteenth birthday, she was not with her father and brothers.

Listening to the low murmurs around her, Isobel touched the perfectly circular black onyx stone her father had given her on her seventh birthday. It had been her mother's necklace, and when she had died in childbirth, Father had taken it and kept it with him always until he had gifted it to Isobel. This stone had given her strength in her darkest hours at the nunnery. It had always reminded her that she was not alone, that she had a father and brothers who loved her, and that one day they would be together. When that time came, she would also finally meet her sisters.

She bit down on her trembling lips. She was now the Brigid heiress. No more was she to be kept safe from those who might try to seize her and bind her in marriage. She had never understood all the terms of her inheritance from her grandmother, but she did remember Father saying she would not inherit the castle if she was wed before she was eighteen. Father had also vowed that on the day she turned eighteen, he and her brothers would personally come for her and bring her home.

Isobel shivered, not from the draft in the chapel but from fear. Her father had not come. Her brothers had not come. Strangers had plucked her from her bed and forced her to ride through day and night, then the next day and night. They had claimed it was at her father's request. They had claimed it was by his bidding. But they had lied. They had brought her to the home she had often dreamed of living in, but neither her father nor her brothers were there. Deception floated in the air.

Her heartbeat tripled its pace as her stepmother stopped whispering furiously to the priest and they both looked at her. Isobel pressed a damp palm to the gown her father had given her as a birthday gift the year before. Father had told her then that she must always be strong and courageous, just as he'd had to be when he brought her to the nunnery and sacrificed his own personal desire to have her live with him so that he could keep her safe. She had vowed to him that she would be, and she would not break that vow now.

She took a deep breath just as the chapel door creaked open and a tall man filled the doorway. A hard knot of dread formed in her belly as she studied the man. His hair was black as a starless night, and his lips twisted in a way that reminded Isobel of how Sister Beatrice's lips always turned down in a grimace. But it was his gray, flat eyes that made Isobel's stomach clench. There was no light of life in his eyes, only a coldness that made him appear devoid of emotion.

The man strode into the room with hard steps, and suspicion swirled within her. Whoever this man was, he commanded respect, or mayhap fear, given the tight faces of the others in the chapel. He came to stand directly in front of her, towering over her so that she took an involuntary step back, only to be shoved forward by Jean as she walked up to Isobel's side.

Isobel tensed as Jean moved closer and speared her with a frosty look. "Isobel, this is Lord Jamie MacLeod. He is the man ye will marry this night."

Isobel's lips parted. *MacLeod?* She swept her gaze over the foreboding man who carried the name of the clan that was her father's greatest foe. Once the shock of a MacLeod standing in front of her sank in, another swept over her. *Marry?* Had Jean truly said Isobel was to marry this man? And this night? She went rigid. Her father, laird of the Campbell clan, would never agree to marry her to a MacLeod and into the clan that had stolen from him.

Liars! She was surrounded by enemies. Jean may be her stepmother and these men may be her father's, but something was amiss. She could feel it in her bones. She did not know Jean. She did not know her father's men. She did not even know the woman hovering in the corner with watchful eyes, the one who Isobel had been told was her half sister.

What she *did* know with undeniable truth was that her father hated the MacLeods and would never bind her in marriage to them.

Tilting up her chin and choosing her words with care, she said, "I'll nae marry anyone without speaking to my father. I must ken his desires." It was best to leave the rest of her feelings unsaid. Her father would understand that she wished to marry an honorable man like him, one whom she loved and who loved her, just as her father had loved her mother.

"This *is* his wish," Jean said in a voice that did not display a hint of warmth or yielding.

Isobel pressed her lips together. "So ye say," she responded. "But I'd hear it from my father's own mouth. I must marry wisely."

And not to a hated enemy.

Jean snorted. "Ye fool. Nae a body present dunnae ken the importance of the choice of husband for ye, as he will rule Brigid Castle."

Isobel sucked in a sharp breath. She was no fool! She knew the man she married one day would hold her castle, yet that was secondary in her mind. If she married for love and the man was honorable, fierce, and loyal to the Campbells, then Brigid Castle would be in excellent hands.

Beside Jean, Lord MacLeod shifted, drawing Isobel's attention. He narrowed his eyes upon her. "Did they nae teach ye proper obedience at the nunnery?" he snarled. "Ye will marry as yer stepmother has bid, or ye will learn what it means to attempt to defy me." His hand curled into a fist.

Isobel's thoughts spun in her head as she stared at the fresh, jagged, red cut running from his right eye to his lip. Had he received that in battle with warriors, or had he received the wound from some poor woman who had been trying to protect herself from him? Isobel swept her gaze around the room, seeing only fear. She'd find no aid from anyone in this room. She had no notion what her stepmother was up to, but Isobel could not believe that the father she knew would marry her to a man without at least telling her himself.

Beyond that, she knew her father would not marry her to a man who threatened to beat her. She had to think no further than the memory of Sister Beatrice, whom he'd sent from the nunnery after learning of her abuse toward Isobel. She'd been afraid to tell him for many years, as Sister Beatrice had sworn it was Isobel's penance for being sinful, but when she had turned eight and her father had visited, he had seen the fresh cuts and Isobel had divulged the truth.

Sister Beatrice had been sent away that very day. Father was her greatest defender. No, it could not be his wish for her to marry this man.

Mayhap her stepmother was trying to make an allegiance with this MacLeod to thwart Father somehow. Isobel did not know. What she did understand was that Father had told her time and again to trust only him and her half brothers because all others would attempt to use her.

She stiffened her spine and notched up her chin. "I will nae agree to marry this night."

A low growl came from Lord MacLeod. Out of the corner of her eye, Isobel saw the priest cross himself, and the hairs on the back of her neck prickled.

Lord MacLeod clutched her arm in an unforgiving vise. "It will bring me great pleasure to gain yer agreement, Isobel."

Fear raced across her skin as he squeezed her arm with such force that she had to bite her cheek to keep from whimpering. She glanced toward the window and out at the dark night. She swallowed hard. Bad things happened at night. Her mother had died at night. Her father had always departed from their visits when the sky was black. Colin, her oldest and favorite brother, had told her on his most recent visit with Father that the MacLeods had defeated them in an important battle on a night when the moon had refused to shine.

Her heart pounded as she scanned the small room for something to offer her reprieve. Her eyes met the piercing blue ones of her half sister, Marsaili. Colin and Findlay had said the girl was dim-witted, yet her eyes looked clear to Isobel. Judging by the woman's unkempt appearance, she needed a rescuer from Jean, too. Clearly, the horrid woman did not properly care for her daughter when Father was not in residence.

Isobel's heart twisted for the young woman, and then an idea came to her. She hated to use Marsaili, but she was desperate and the woman would not be hurt. Isobel placed a hand on Lord MacLeod's arm and forced herself to smile up at him. "My lord, forgive me. I am sorry for moments ago. If I'm to be married, please may I have my sister Marsaili by my side—washed of the dirt covering her, of course."

Lord MacLeod stared down at Isobel with an implacable gaze that made her stomach tighten. He was going to refute her request; she simply knew it.

"Ye wish the half-wit to be yer witness?" he asked incredulously as he released her.

"I do, my lord," she replied, struggling to control her anger at his referring to Marsaili as a half-wit. Isobel looked at Marsaili, who, much to her surprise, appeared to be scrutinizing Isobel. She smiled at Marsaili, hoping to ease her fears should there be any.

And that's when all hell unleashed.

The motto of the MacLeod clan, *Hold fast*, strummed a relentless beat through Graham MacLeod's head as he stood in the pitch-black woods that surrounded Innis Chonnell Castle. Revenge was not far off; all he had to do was wait. He stared into the night methodically, recalling what he and his men had learned of their enemy's routine in the two days since arriving on the island and hiding in the thick woods.

By now, all the Campbells had long been to bed. There were five guards spaced evenly apart on each of the north, south, east, and west walls that surrounded the castle, yet not a one of them had seen Graham or his men as they had swum through the loch to reach the island, made camp in the woods, and even scaled the fortress wall in rehearsal for their revenge. The Campbell men who had been left to guard Innis Chonnell were not very observant. This both surprised and pleased him.

He was here for two reasons: to destroy their castle, and to take Isobel Campbell, the laird's daughter and the new heiress to Brigid Castle. That castle was a key holding for the king and for the MacLeods who would be protecting him from their enemies. He pictured Brigid in his mind, sitting dauntingly between Skye and the mainland. All ships had to pass by that castle to get to Skye, and they had to have the permission of the keeper of Brigid to do so. Currently, that keeper was Isobel Campbell's grandmother. His mouth tugged at the corners in a respectful smile. The older woman was cunning. She had cleverly orchestrated a system in which her men placed a chain in the water that ran from the shores of Brigid to the shores of the mainland, and she ordered that chain raised against those ships she did not want to let pass. The ships would then have to turn back and attempt the stormy passages of the Minch to reach their destinations.

King David would be well pleased to marry Isobel to someone of his choosing, someone who would hold Brigid Castle and strengthen the king's ability to maintain his rightful position as King of Scots, and Graham was well pleased to deliver her to the king as promised and take a step toward the destruction of the Campbells for their many crimes against his family.

Harnessing the anger the mere thought of the Campbells always brought, Graham repeatedly squeezed his hands into tight fists and released them until they prickled and burned, warding off the numbness trying to set in from the cold as he also took deep breaths of freezing air to keep his mind sharp. It would not be long now, and he needed to be ready. Isobel had arrived at the castle hours earlier, exactly as their informant had told them a sennight before that she would. Soon the informant would signal them to attack.

With a glance toward the forest, where he knew his men attempted to rest before battle, he listened. He could not see his men, but their even breathing filled the silence with a blanketing *whoosh* that told him they were near and in clusters. Snores punctuated the rhythmic inhalations and exhalations. He envied them. He could never settle his mind enough to sleep before a battle.

Gripping his sword, each muscle rippled down the length of his arm in response. Physically, he was ready. He had never been in better condition in his life. He shifted his weight to the leg that he had injured over a year earlier when he'd fought against English knights trying to seize his eldest brother Iain's wife, Marion. The only pain Graham felt now was from the tightness of muscles needing warmth. He smiled grimly. Relentless, excruciating training had rid him of every trace of the limp the near-fatal wound had plagued him with for many months following. He had the strength of a warrior to match the best.

It wasn't boastful, just a fact he had proven by testing himself against both his older brothers, Iain and Lachlan, who were legendary fighters. Finally, he had honed his body into that of a combatant equal to both his brothers. Gratitude filled him. While the attempt had begun as a result of jealousy toward Lachlan and a need to best him, that desire no longer plagued him. He prayed now that his strength in mind was as great as that of his sword arm, for tonight he would need both.

Feeling restless, Graham signaled to his younger brother, Cameron. "I'm going to run through the course of attack once more," he said in a low whisper so as not to disturb the sleeping men.

"Again?" Cameron replied with a snort. "Do ye nae believe the forty times before committed the course to yer memory?"

"There is always opportunity to improve," Graham replied, smiling into the darkness and choosing not to scold his brother for his impertinent tone. He was glad to have Cameron with him for this battle, impertinence and all. He trusted no one in this world more than Cameron, who Graham was closer to than he was to Iain or Lachlan. Though Graham would die to protect any of them, Cameron had always been his confidant. Iain, as laird of the clan, had always kept himself somewhat distant, and Graham's relationship with Lachlan had been strained for many years due to his own folly. But he did not want to dwell now on how foolish he had been. He would have the rest of his life—he hoped—to try to make amends for that.

"We kinnae afford an error, Brother. If we make one, dunnae fool yerself into believing we will get this chance again. The Campbell will nae be so foolish as to leave Innis Chonnell guarded by so few of his men whilst the rest are away fighting, and Isobel Campbell will be married to our enemy before we can even escape this island."

"Ye're right, Brother. Do ye want me to make the sweep with ye?" Cameron asked in hushed tones.

"Nay. Ye take respite. I'll go alone and whistle if I see trouble."

"Ye're certain?"

Graham could hear the weariness in his brother's tone. "Aye. I'm certain. I'll nae be long." He didn't wait for Cameron to respond this time. He merely turned and plodded through the thick snow, listening to the howling wolves that prowled the woods. His fatigued legs burned as he walked. He was weary. They all were. They'd ridden at a relentless pace from their home on the Isle of Skye to Loch Awe, but it had been necessary to arrive here, where they knew Isobel was being brought to marry his and Cameron's uncle Jamie, the traitor.

Burning rage warmed him at the thought of his uncle. Graham smirked into the darkness. It would give him great pleasure to snatch Isobel Campbell from his uncle. Graham's informant had told him that Jamie was to marry the heiress, and Graham felt sure Jamie thought to use marriage to Isobel to assure the Campbell's continued aid in his attempt to steal the lairdship of the MacLeod clan from Iain. And the Campbell thought to use the marriage of his daughter to Jamie to assure Jamie oversaw Brigid as the Campbell himself wished, which meant using the castle to help them control the Isles and seize the throne from King David. Destroying Innis Chonnell tonight and taking Isobel would obliterate much of the enemy's plan.

A sudden howling nearby drew Graham's attention back to his surroundings. So far they had not had to contend with the wolves, and he said a quick prayer that their luck held, preferably for the duration of their time on the island. But if God was not feeling so very generous this night, hopefully the wolves would at least stay away until after Graham and his men stormed the castle and had seized Isobel Campbell. The best way to fight off the wolves was fire, but if he could see the castle wall from where they were, then the Campbell men would surely be able to see a fire, so such an approach would be impossible.

He shoved branches out of his way as he walked, but one snapped back too quickly for him to duck and it sliced his cheek. The instant warmth of blood trickled down his icy skin, the contrast of hot and cold making him grit his teeth. Ignoring the sting of the cut, he wiped the blood away with the back of his hand and kept moving toward the embankment where they would scale the fortress wall into the castle courtyard. He had learned a long time ago that pain, whether to the heart or the body, could be harnessed—sometimes even conquered—with a strong enough will.

His will was as deep as the ocean, and its current flowed only toward revenge. Coming to the embankment, he stared up at the looming castle. His heart began to pound as his blood rushed through his veins, sending painful pricks of anticipation to every part of his body.

Suddenly, a woman's scream split the silent night. *"Ban-druidh, ban-druidh!"*

The word *witch* rang loud and clear. The signal had been given. It was time to pilfer the prize he had promised his brothers and his king.

Isobel could do no more than stand there stupefied as Marsaili screeched at the top of her lungs.

"Ban-druidh, ban-druidh, ban-druidh!" she cried while pointing at Isobel.

Isobel stared in shock and horror as Jean slapped Marsaili across the face, but it did not stop the woman's screams.

Her face red with fury, Jean motioned to two men

standing guard at the door. "Take her from the chapel!" Jean snapped, one hand gripping Marsaili's arm so tight that Jean's fingers became white. Her stepmother looked to the priest and barked, "Marry them!"

Fear propelled Isobel to scramble backward, but she ran into someone. Glancing over her shoulder, a wave of dismay filled her at the sight of Jamie MacLeod. He shoved her forward so violently that she nearly fell to her knees, only catching herself with a hand to the wall.

"Ye heard yer mistress, Father. Marry me to the wench right now," he said, moving directly behind her as if to block her from fleeing, which she intended to do as soon as she could determine how.

"But if she be a witch—" the priest started, the rest of his sentence drowned out by Marsaili's wailing.

Lord MacLeod pushed by Isobel as he strode toward the priest, whose eyes went round as he cowered. At that exact moment, the guards dragged Marsaili past Isobel, but the woman grasped onto Isobel's arm and began to drag Isobel with her. As Isobel worked to free herself from the painful grip of her half sister, who was now kicking one guard and clawing at the other—all while still managing to hold onto Isobel and move them toward the door—more shouting came from behind her.

"Ye will marry us!" Lord MacLeod boomed.

"But, my lord, if the lady be a witch—"

"Ban-druidh, ban-druidh," Marsaili chanted.

"If ye dunnae shut that loon's mouth, I'll kill her," Lord MacLeod snarled to the guards who gripped Marsaili.

Isobel struggled to block out the noise in the chapel and the noise in her head. She had to think. She had to flee. She didn't know why Jean was trying to marry her to this man, but he was clearly evil. Her father would never have agreed to such a match, which explained why they were trying to force her into it now, when her father and her brothers were not present.

"Just take them both out!" Jean demanded as the guards struggled to fight off a now spitting, snarling Marsaili while trying to get her to release Isobel. With a hard yank, Isobel found herself jerked outside into the freezing, black night along with Marsaili.

"Ban-druidh, ban-druidh," Marsaili screamed so loudly it hurt Isobel's ears.

With a loud bang, the chapel door slammed shut behind them.

Marsaili immediately fell quiet, and one of the guards stomped away only to come back seconds later with a torch that pierced the darkness with a small bit of light. It was just enough that when the guard shone it in Marsaili's face, Isobel started at what she saw. Marsaili was giving her the sweetest smile.

Then she released Isobel. "Ye're welcome," she said, batting one of the guards' hands away while staring straight at Isobel.

Isobel blinked. "Ye were lying in order to help me?" Isobel whispered, both grateful and astounded.

Marsaili winked at her as she shifted her gaze past the guards and Isobel. "The fit has passed," she announced. Isobel looked behind her at the wall that surrounded the castle, but she saw nothing abnormal. She had no notion what her half sister was staring at.

When she turned back around, Marsaili dragged her gaze to Isobel and then the guards. "I vow to be verra good. Ye can move away now. I will nae leave."

The guards exchanged a wary look but nodded and stepped far enough back to give them some solitude, but not so far that they could not easily and quickly take Marsaili in hand again if necessary.

Marsaili stepped closer to Isobel and grabbed her by the hand. "Dunnae fear," the woman whispered. "Ye'll nae be marrying that devil Jamie MacLeod this night."

Relief made Isobel tremble. She squeezed Marsaili's hand. "I kenned well Father would nae marry me to his greatest enemy," she replied in hushed tones. Isobel swallowed hard, trying to think how to delicately say the rest of what was in her mind. "Marsaili," she said gently, "is yer mother…" She paused. How did one ask someone if her mother was evil? *Och!* There was no good way. With a quick breath, she asked, "Is Jean conspiring with Lord MacLeod?"

Marsaili's eyes popped wide. "Aye." She quirked her mouth for a moment, and then said, "Conspiracy blankets everything, Isobel, but nae all of it be born of evil."

Isobel frowned. "Are ye trying to tell me that more people are conspiring against our father?"

"Aye," Marsaili replied, her gaze moving past Isobel once more.

"What are ye looking at?" Isobel demanded.

"Hush," Marsaili hissed. "Ye will attract the fools' attention."

Isobel glanced toward the guards who were facing each other and talking, then she looked back to Marsaili, who shifted from foot to foot as if anxious. A warning sounded in her head, and she whipped around and glanced toward the top of the wall where men stood on guard. Slowly, she crept her gaze along the wall as Marsaili began to tug on her arm.

"Turn around, Isobel," Marsaili commanded, but Isobel ignored her as the warning in her head grew almost deafening. She counted five guards on each wall before

Marsaili pulled her around with a jerk.

Isobel gasped at her half sister, and craned her neck to look behind her once more. Four guards! There were but four guards to the north. As she stared it became three, then two, then one, and then the wall was bare of guards. For a moment, she was not certain she could believe her eyes, but then the same thing occurred on the south wall. She sucked in a breath, turned toward Marsaili, and asked in a low voice, "Do ye stand with Father or against him?"

Isobel didn't know what was happening, but she knew her stepmother and Lord MacLeod were evil, and Marsaili had been the only person willing to help her thus far. She didn't know if she could trust Marsaili, but she knew she could not trust Jean or Lord MacLeod, and it seemed her father's men were currently doing Jean's bidding.

Marsaili locked gazes with Isobel. "I stand with ye, Isobel. I vow it."

Isobel's heart thudded in her ears, and she faced the wall once more. As the moon came out from behind a cloud, a very large, very powerful-appearing, half-naked man poised for battle with a sword in hand became silhouetted against the night. Her breath caught in her throat. Suddenly, he disappeared, dropping over the wall so quickly she would almost have questioned that she'd seen anything at all except another man scrambled over the wall, and then another, and another. Isobel didn't know whether to scream in warning at an attack or sigh with relief at a rescue.

Marsaili gripped her shoulder from behind. "They are here to help us."

Uncertainty froze Isobel as she stared at the largest man. The darkness obscured his features, but she could see him raise a finger to his lips in a motion for her to be silent.

Before she could decide what to do, one of the guards

yelled, "Attack!"

At the same moment, something *swished* by her ear. And then again. *Swish.*

The guard's shouts abruptly stopped, and then a *thud* resounded in the night, followed quickly by another.

She did not have to turn around to know Jean's men were dead. Knots of fear formed in her belly as Marsaili moved to Isobel's side and gripped her hand. Marsaili squeezed her fingers hard as the giant of a man she had been watching at the top of the wall came to a shuddering stop in front of them. Twenty men flanked his sides like a human wall of iron. Something about his presence commanded attention above all else. His cold, hard gaze did not offer comfort but only more fear.

"Isobel Campbell?" he asked with such contempt that she immediately took a step back.

She glanced to Marsaili for reassurance but saw a flash of guilt on her half sister's face. "Ye deceived me?" Isobel asked and accused at once.

Marsaili bit her lip. "'Tis nae so simple, Isobel. Please, I mean ye no harm. I only seek to help ye. Ye must trust me!"

"Intruders!" a voice rang from the rampart.

A horn blasted, and before Isobel could respond, the giant swept her and Marsaili behind him. "Neil! Defend them with yer life," he called to one of his men.

She was seized by strong hands and dragged to the side of the keep, along with Marsaili. The chapel door banged open, a whistle pierced the air, and men suddenly flooded into the courtyard from the main castle.

Besieged by doubt, Isobel stood by the man Neil and

watched the battle. Her father's men—they wore his plaid but did he have their loyalty?—fought against the men Marsaili had vowed were there to help them. Isobel's heart raced as two warriors drew near.

Neil pushed her head toward the ground. "Stay low," he commanded.

She bumped foreheads with Marsaili, and as swords clanked above them, Marsaili grasped her hands. "Whatever happens, stay with me," Marsaili said.

Dismay filled Isobel's chest. Had she made the best choice? Did she even have one? Cries filled the courtyard along with the hard clank of steel meeting steel. The heat of at least fifty bodies drenched in sweat obliterated the biting cold in the air. Men rushed by her toward one another and bumped into her. She looked to where Neil had been, only to realize he was no longer beside her. Instead he was fighting before her, protecting her and Marsaili.

She stood abruptly, bringing her half sister with her. Two men battled very near, and the taller of the two—a Campbell—lunged forward in an attempt to plunge his sword into a bald-headed intruder, but he missed and his blade sliced through the skirt of Isobel's gown. The soldier's eyes caught hers, and the desire to kill shining there made panic riot within her. This man was crazed with the need to kill, and she feared greatly she was about to be a casualty.

"Yer laird is my father!" she screamed, hoping to pierce through the haze that had descended upon the man, or perchance remind him where his loyalty should lie.

His answer was a jerk of his sword, which released her gown so that she had barely enough time to scramble backward against the hard stone wall just as her father's soldier was cut down by the man he had been fighting. The Campbell man fell at her feet, and the bald-headed marauder who had killed him didn't spare her or Marsaili a glance. He simply disappeared into the press of bodies, and Isobel stood shaking, taking a few deep gulps of air only to realize it was heavy with smoke.

As coughs wracked Isobel's body, Marsaili tugged on her arm. "Isobel, I fear the men who came to help us will not triumph. We must flee!"

"Flee?" Isobel cried out, trying to stifle the building panic. "To where? Do ye ken where Father is? Or Findlay and Colin?"

Marsaili gaped at her for a moment but finally answered. "Aye. Come with me."

Isobel looked around the courtyard, which was splintered with early-morning light, a haze of smoke having replaced the oppressive darkness. One glance toward the castle confirmed what she had suspected: it was on fire.

The hairs on the back of her neck prickled as she stared at Marsaili's outstretched hand. "Why are these men burning our father's castle?"

When Marsaili opened and shut her mouth as if she did not know what to say, Isobel's uneasiness grew. "Who are these men?" she tried.

Instead of answering, Marsaili grabbed Isobel's arm and began to tug her along the wall. Isobel dug in her heels and yanked back, but Marsaili was a head taller and a bit heavier.

"Marsaili!" Isobel yelled over the noise of battle. "Who are these men?" she asked again.

Marsaili stopped at the beginning of a narrow path that led to a small door built into the wall. The passage was blocked by Lord MacLeod, who was fighting the large man who had asked if she was Isobel Campbell. A strangled cry came from Marsaili as she glanced between the path and the melee they had left behind them in the courtyard.

Gripping Isobel hard, Marsaili stared at her. "Ye have been deceived, Isobel."

The desperate, pleading look on her face shocked Isobel. "By whom?" she whispered, her thoughts spinning. "Ye or someone else?"

Tears filled Marsaili's eyes. "By Father, by Findlay, and by Colin, when he was alive."

"What?" Isobel moaned, twisting her wrist to try to escape, but Marsaili held her more tightly. "Colin is dead? Our brother is dead?"

"Aye… And by me," Marsaili sobbed.

Fright swept over Isobel, and she yanked her wrist away from Marsaili. "Ye killed our brother?"

"Nay!" Marsaili cried out as tears flowed down her face. "I have *deceived* ye, but I vow it was to help ye. And now we are trapped." She motioned to Lord MacLeod and the other man. "We must get around them somehow!"

"I'm nae going anywhere with ye," Isobel replied, scrambling backward to ensure she was out of Marsaili's reach. But her half sister did not make a move to grab for her.

Marsaili swiped at the tears wetting her cheeks. "I dunnae blame ye for nae trusting me, but if ye stay, ye will be married to Lord MacLeod. Do ye wish that?"

Icy fear twisted through her. "Nay," she whispered.

Marsaili held out her hand. "There are enemies all around ye, Isobel, but I'm nae one of them."

Isobel's stomach clenched as she looked past Marsaili to the two men blocking the path. They circled each other, and then their swords met in a wide arc over their heads. The larger man's forearms and biceps seemed to strain against his skin as he fought Lord MacLeod. With a roar that made gooseflesh rise on Isobel's arms, he pushed Lord MacLeod's sword down and out of his hands, and shoved the man backward. Lord MacLeod stumbled to his knees.

"Come!" Marsaili shouted, already moving past the men.

Not seeing any choice but to follow, Isobel stepped forward, but the men's plaids caught her attention and she froze. They were identical!

But that would mean they were from the same clan…

Her heart pounded furiously. The bigger man swung his sword down to deliver a blow to Lord MacLeod. Isobel watched in horror as Marsaili started back for her, and at the same time, Lord MacLeod sprang up and jerked Marsaili in front of him as the shining steel blade came down.

"Nay!" Isobel shouted, and the tall, muscled warrior pulled his blade back just enough that only its tip met with Marsaili's clothing. Her gown parted, but her skin was untouched. Before Isobel could release a breath of relief, Lord MacLeod whipped out a dagger and dug the point into Marsaili's throat. A drop of crimson immediately appeared, dread tightening Isobel's chest. Lord MacLeod was a bad, bad man.

As if to prove her right and stoke the flame of her tension, he said, "Set down yer weapon, Nephew, or I'll kill this dim-witted wench here and now."

Nephew! Isobel gaped at the stranger, who she could now see clearly in the light of day. He had warm, golden-brown eyes and wavy, gleaming, chestnut hair that just grazed the top of his shoulders. He wore a mask of indifference, but a vein beat a rapid pulse at his neck. She could hardly believe a man who belonged to the clan of her family's greatest enemy would set down his weapon to save a Campbell, but his gaze flicked from his uncle to Marsaili to the dagger.

A slow, menacing smile pulled at his lips. "Ye may take me captive if I set down my weapon, but ye will nae save the castle. It burns even as we stand here, and ye and the Campbell will nae be able to use it to provide shelter for the men ye train for evil any longer."

Isobel's breath caught. *Evil!* Her father would never train men for evil purposes! This man was mistaken.

"I'll nae need it," Lord MacLeod responded and glanced at Isobel. "Ye may congratulate me, Nephew. I'm to marry Isobel Campbell here, and her inheritance, Brigid Castle, will be mine."

Isobel seethed. "I'd rather be dead than married to a MacLeod," she spat.

Lord MacLeod narrowed his eyes upon her and gave her a look that told her he'd be all too happy to kill her once he had her castle. The other man, Lord MacLeod's nephew, offered an amused smile.

"Graham!" yelled a voice from a distance. "Two Campbell ships approach!"

Hope swelled in Isobel's chest. Perchance her father or brother was arriving!

"We must away," the man in the distance called. "The main keep burns steady, and the enemy has been felled. Deal quickly with our treacherous uncle. Our work here is done. I've sent the rest of the men on."

Confusion battered Isobel. The MacLeods were apparently a clan at war with itself, but Lord MacLeod seemed the evil one with his dagger still pressed to Marsaili's neck, and the other man—this *Graham*—seemed to be the one with a sense of honor.

"Dunnae listen to yer brother, my nephew, and set down yer weapon!" Lord MacLeod boomed and then ran his blade across Marsaili's neck just hard enough to draw a line of blood. Marsaili whimpered, and Isobel had to bite hard on her lip so she would not cry out, too. Her gut told her that Graham was Marsaili's only hope. Even if it was her father or Findlay approaching, she feared they would not reach them in time to help.

Isobel watched in astonishment as Graham set down his sword and stood with his arms spread wide. "Release the woman, ye coward, and face me like a man."

"Graham!" his brother called from the distance again.

"Go, Cameron!" Graham shouted in reply. "I'll meet ye where we arrived, and if I dunnae and the sun is high in the sky, leave me until the bird calls once again in the night."

Isobel could not believe this stranger before her. Either he was mad or he had no doubt he could cut down his uncle. He had his gaze trained in the distance and, after a moment, tension seeped from Graham's face. She suspected it was because his brother had departed safely. She inhaled a startled breath to see such a display of caring from her family's enemy. Her father and brothers had described them as beasts, but this man was showing nothing but bravery and honor. He had bid his brother to leave him in order to ensure his safety and willingly faced his uncle without aid to protect Marsaili. Isobel could not help but admire his selflessness, but at the same time, she felt as if she was betraying her father and brother.

She focused on Lord MacLeod just as he shoved Marsaili away from him and toward Graham, who caught her as she started to fall and drew her up to her feet. Before Isobel could discern what Lord MacLeod was conspiring to achieve, the dagger flew from his hands and straight toward Marsaili.

Isobel screamed a warning, but there was no need.

Graham pushed Marsaili out of the way, and the dagger hit him in his sword arm. He winced, then reached up and ripped the dagger from his flesh as Lord MacLeod started toward him with his own sword now in hand.

By the burning hatred in Graham's eyes, Isobel didn't doubt that he would defeat Lord MacLeod, even wounded and weaponless, but suddenly shouts filled the courtyard and the ground beneath her vibrated from the thunderous sound of running men. Glancing behind her to see who was approaching, her heart leaped at the sea of men wearing her father's plaid as they rushed toward her.

"'Tis Findlay!" Marsaili shouted, but the absence of relief and presence of fear made Isobel frown.

An almost-inhuman roar came from Graham, and he barreled past Lord MacLeod, elbowing his uncle in the face as he went, then charged full force at Findlay. But from the left and the right, her father's men swarmed toward Graham.

"Dunnae kill him!" Lord MacLeod shouted, his voice gurgling from the blood pouring from his nose. "He is mine to deal with!"

Isobel's thoughts raced and spun as she stared, stupefied and half in fear for the warrior who had saved Marsaili's life. Even with one of her father's men grasping his left arm now and another holding his right, Graham continued to move toward Findlay with astonishing strength, dragging her father's men with him. Findlay, sword in hand with a shockingly cruel smile twisting his lips, strode toward Graham. "How is yer sister, MacLeod? How is my bonny bride?"

Isobel gulped a breath of utter astonishment. Findlay was married to a MacLeod? She frowned. She did not understand. Then Marsaili's words echoed in Isobel's head:

Ye have been deceived. Surely she could trust her brother, couldn't she?

Findlay sent the hilt of his sword into Graham's forehead, and the man slumped forward, unconscious. Isobel trembled as she watched his sudden dead weight cause the men clutching him to stagger and almost fall. Graham had sacrificed himself honorably to save Marsaili, and in truth, Isobel felt numb and confused rather than relieved.

Marsaili took Isobel's hand. "The devil's come home," she whispered, her wide gaze fixed on Findlay.

Before Isobel could question her half sister's comment, Lord MacLeod jerked her away from Marsaili and toward him. "Time for us to marry, Isobel."

Isobel looked to Findlay. "Brother, surely Father dunnae wish me to marry a MacLeod?"

The look of contempt he gave her felt like a slap across the face. "Ye dunnae ken a thing, Isobel, and ye nae ever have. Father wished it that way. Ye will do as ye're told and marry Jamie MacLeod this night."

"I will nae!" she exclaimed, flinching when Findlay strode toward her, his face twisted with rage. She half expected Marsaili to abandon her grip on Isobel and move out of Findlay's reach, but he closed the distance between them in a breath, shoved Marsaili away, and gripped Isobel hard by the arms. "Ye will do as ye're told," he growled again.

"Findlay, please," she said on a rush of fear. "Ye're hurting me."

"Let her go!" Marsaili cried out, thrashing at Findlay's arm.

When Findlay backhanded Marsaili and she fell to her knees, Isobel flinched and tried to help her. Findlay jerked Isobel back. "Leave her," he demanded. "She's nae worthy of yer pity."

Disbelief struck Isobel momentarily mute. This was a side of her brother she had never seen. He had never been as warm to her as Father or Colin had, but he had never seemed *cruel*. Pity twisted inside her chest and made her eyes fill with tears as she looked at Marsaili, who was struggling to stand. When Isobel focused on Findlay once more, he smirked at her as if he understood something, but she could not imagine what.

"It seems ye inherited yer mother's weakness of compassion, Isobel. 'Tis a shame for ye, but a good thing for me. Listen well. Ye will marry Lord MacLeod this night, or Marsaili will suffer for it. I may nae be able to touch ye, per Father's orders, but I *will* beat Marsaili to her death if ye dunnae do as I say."

With that, Findlay roared, "Bring the damned priest out here now!"

Dear Readers,

I invite you to try My Fair Duchess (A Once Upon a Rogue Novel, Book 1)

Prologue

The Year of Our Lord 1795
St. Ives, Cambridgeshire, England

The day Colin Sinclair, the Marquess of Nortingham and the future Duke of Aversley, entered the world, he brought nothing but havoc with him.

The Duchess of Aversley's birthing screams filled Waverly House, accompanied by the relentless pattering of rain that beat against the large glass window of Alexander Sinclair's study. The current Duke of Aversley gripped the edge of his desk, the wood digging into his palms. He did not know how much more he could take or how much longer he could acquiesce to his wife's refusal of his request to be present in the birthing room. He knew his wish was unusual and that she feared what he saw would dampen his desire for her, but nothing would ever do that.

Camilla's hoarse voice sliced through the silence again and fed the festering fear that filled him. She might die from this.

The possibility made him tremble. Why hadn't he controlled his lust? After six failed attempts to give him a child,

Camilla's body was weak. He'd known the truth but had chosen to ignore it. Moisture dampened his silk shirt, and Camilla screeched once more. He shook his head, trying to ward off the sound.

He reached across his desk, and with a pounding heart and trembling hand, he slid the crystal decanter toward him. If he did not do something to calm his nerves, he would bolt straight out of this room and barge into their bedchamber. The last thing he wanted to do was cause Camilla undue anxiety. The Scotch lapped over the edge of the tumbler as he poured it, dripping small droplets of liquor on the contracts he had been blindly staring at for the last four hours.

He did not make a move to rescue the papers as the ink blurred. He did not give a goddamn about the papers. All he cared about was Camilla. The physician's previous words of warning that the duchess should not try for an heir again played repeatedly through Alexander's mind. The words grew in volume as the storm raged outside and his wife's shrieks tore through the mansion.

Alexander could have lived a thousand lifetimes without an heir, but he was a weak fool. He craved Camilla, body and soul. His desire, along with his pompous certainty that everything would eventually turn out all right for them because he was the duke, had caused him to ignore the physician and eagerly yield to his wife's fervent wish to have a child.

As Camilla's high, keening wails vibrated the air around him, he gripped his glass a fraction harder. The crystal cracked, cutting his hand with razor-like precision. He yanked off his cravat and wrapped it around his bleeding hand. Lightning split the shadows in the room with bright, blinding light, followed by his study door crashing open and

Camilla's sister, Jane, flying through the entrance. Her red hair streamed out behind her, tears running down her face.

"The physician says come now. Camilla's—" Jane's voice cracked. She dashed a hand across her wet cheeks and moved across the room and around the desk to stand behind his chair. She placed a hand on his shoulder. "Camilla is dying. The doctor needs you to tell him whether to try to save her or the baby."

Pain, the likes of which the duke had never experienced, sliced through his chest and curled in his belly. A fierce cramp immediately seized him. "What sort of choice is that?" he cried as he stood.

Jane nodded sympathetically, then simply turned and motioned him to follow her. With effort, he forced his numb legs to move up the stairs toward his wife's moans. With every step, his heartbeat increased until he was certain it would pound out of his chest. He could not live without her, yet he knew she would not want to live without the babe. If he told the doctor to save her over their child, she would hate him, and misery would continue to plague her and chafe as it had done every time she had lost a babe these past six years.

He could not cause her such pain, but he could not pick the child over her. Outside the bedchamber door, Jane paused and turned to him, her face splotchy. "What are you going to do? I must know to prepare myself."

Alexander had never been a praying man, despite the fact that his mother had been a devout believer and had tried to get him to be one, as well. His father and grandfather had always said Aversley dukes made their own fates and only weak men looked to a higher power to grant them favors and exceptions. Alexander stiffened. He was a stupid fool who had thought himself more powerful than God.

The day his mother had died, she had told him that one day, he would have to pay for this sin.

Was today the day? Alexander drew in a long, shuddering breath, mind racing. What could he do? He would renounce every conviction he held dear to keep his wife and child.

Squeezing his eyes shut, he made a vow to God. If He would save Camilla and the babe, he would pray every day and seek God's wisdom in all things. Surely, this penance would suffice.

A blood-curdling scream split the silence. Alexander's heart exploded as he shoved past Jane and threw the door open. The cream-colored sheets of their bed, now soaked crimson, lay scattered on the dark hardwood floor. Camilla, appearing incredibly small, twisted and whimpered in the center of the gigantic four-poster. Her once-white lacy gown was bunched at her waist to expose her slender legs, and Alexander winced at the blood smeared across her normally olive skin.

Moving toward her, his world tilted. His wife, his Camilla, stared at him with glazed eyes and cracked lips. A deathly pallor had replaced the healthy flush her face usually held. Blue veins pulsed along the base of her neck, giving her skin a thin, papery appearance. The sour stench of death filled the heavy air.

Only seconds had passed, yet it seemed like much longer. The physician swung toward Alexander. He appeared aged since coming through the door hours before; deep lines marked his forehead, the sides of his eyes, and around his mouth. Normally an impeccably kept man, his hair dangled over his right eye, and his shirt, stained dark red, hung out from his trousers. Shoving his hair out of his eye, the physician asked, "Who do you want me to try to save,

Your Grace?"

Alexander curled his hands into fists by his sides, hissing at the throbbing pain the movement caused his cut palm. His mother's last words echoed in his head: *Great sins require great penance*.

The duke glanced at his wife's face, then slowly slid his gaze to her swollen belly. "Both of them," he responded. Fresh sweat broke out across his forehead as the doctor shook his head.

"The babe is twisted the wrong way. Even if I can get it out, Her Grace will be ripped beyond repair. She'll likely bleed out."

Anger coursed through Alexander's veins. "Both of them," he repeated, his voice shaking.

"If she lives, I'm certain she'll be barren. You are sure?"

"Positive," he snapped, seized by a wave of nausea and a certainty that he had failed to give up enough to save them both. Rushing to Camilla's side, he kneeled and gripped her hand as her back formed a perfect arch and another cry broke past her lips—the loudest scream yet.

Alexander closed his eyes and fervently vowed to God never to touch his wife again if only she and his babe would be allowed to live. He would do this and would keep his sacrifice between God and himself for as long as he drew breath and never tell a living soul of his penance. This time he would heed his mother's warnings. Her threadbare voice filled his head as he murmured her words. "True atonement is between the sinner and God or else it is not true, and the day of reckoning will come more terrible and shattering than imaginable."

Alexander repeated the oath, coldness gripping him and burrowing into his bones.

Moments later, his throat burned, and he could not stop

the tears of happiness and relief that rolled down his face as he cradled his healthy son in his arms.

Then in a faint but happy voice Camilla called out to him. "Alex, come to me," Camilla murmured, gazing at him with shining eyes and raising a willowy arm to beckon him. He froze where he stood and curled his fingers tighter around his swaddled son, desperate to hold on to the joy of seconds ago, and yet the elation slipped away when realizing the promise he had made to God.

That vow had saved his wife and child. As much as he wanted to tell Camilla of it now, as her forehead wrinkled and uncertainty filled her eyes, fear stilled his tongue. What if he told her, and then she died? Or the babe died?

"You've done well, Camilla," he said in a cool tone. The words felt ripped from his gut. Inside, he throbbed, raw and broken.

He handed the babe to Jane and then turned on his heel and quit the room. At the stairs, he gripped the banister for support as he summoned the butler and gave the orders to remove his belongings from the bedchamber he had shared with Camilla since the day they had married.

As he feared, as soon as Camilla was able to, she came to him, desperate and pleading for explanations. Her words seared his heart and branded him with misery. He trembled every time he sent her away from him, and her broken-hearted sobs rang through the halls. The pain that stole her smile and the gleam that had once filled her eyes made him fear for her and for them, but the dreams that dogged him of her death or their son's death should the vow be broken frightened him more. Sleeplessness plagued him, and he took to creeping into his son's nursery, where he would send the nanny away and rock his boy until the wee hours of the morning, pouring all his love into his child.

Days slid into months that turned to the first year and then the second. As his bond with Camilla weakened, his tie to his heir strengthened. Laughter filled Waverly House, but it was only the child's laughter and Alexander's. It seemed to him, the closer he became to his child and the more attention he lavished on him, the larger the wall became between him and Camilla until she reminded him of an angry queen reigning in her mountainous tower of ice. Yet, it was his fault she was there with no hope of rescue.

The night she quit coming to his bedchamber, Alexander thanked God and prayed she would now turn the love he knew was in her to their son, whom she seemed to blame for Alexander's abandonment. He awoke in the morning, and when the nanny brought Colin to Alexander, he decided to carry his son with him to break his fast, in hopes that Camilla would want to hold him. As he entered the room with Colin, she did not smile. Her lips thinned with obvious anger as she excused herself, and he was caught between the wish to cry and the urge to rage at her.

Still, his fingers burned to hold her hand and itched to caress the gentle slope of her cheekbone. Eventually, his skin became cold. His fingers curiously numb. Then one day, sitting across from him at dinner in the silent dining room, Camilla looked at him and he recoiled at the sharp thorns of revenge shining in her eyes.

The following week the Season began, and he dutifully escorted her to the first ball. Knots of tension made his shoulders ache as they walked down the staircase, side by side, so close yet a thousand ballrooms apart. After they were announced, she turned to him and he prepared himself to decline her request to dance.

She raised one eyebrow, her lips curling into a thinly veiled smile of contempt. "Quit cringing, Alexander. You may go to the card room. My dances are all taken, I assure you."

Within moments, she twirled onto the dance floor, first with one gentleman and then another and another until the night faded near to morning. Alexander stood in the shadows, leaning against a column and never moving, aware of the curious looks people cast his way. He was helplessly sure his wife was trying to hurt him, and he silently started to pray she would finally turn all her wrath at how he had changed to him and begin to love the child she had longed for…and for whom she had almost died.

Series by Julie Johnstone

Scottish Medieval Romance Books:

Highlander Vows: Entangled Hearts Series

When a Laird Loves a Lady, Book 1
Wicked Highland Wishes, Book 2
Christmas in the Scot's Arms, Book 3
When a Highlander Loses His Heart, Book 4
When a Highlander Loses His Heart, Book 4
How a Scot Surrenders to a Lady, Book 5

Regency Romance Books:

A Whisper of Scandal Series

Bargaining with a Rake, Book 1
Conspiring with a Rogue, Book 2
Dancing with a Devil, Book 3
After Forever, Book 4
The Dangerous Duke of Dinnisfree, Book 5

A Once Upon A Rogue Series

My Fair Duchess, Book 1
My Seductive Innocent, Book 2
My Enchanting Hoyden, Book 3

Lords of Deception Series

What a Rogue Wants, Book 1

Danby Regency Christmas Novellas

The Redemption of a Dissolute Earl, Book 1

Season For Surrender, Book 2

It's in the Duke's Kiss, Book 3

Regency Anthologies

A Summons from the Duke of Danby (Regency Christmas Summons Book 2)

Thwarting the Duke (When the Duke Comes to Town, Book 2)

Regency Romance Box Sets

Dukes, Duchesses & Dashing Noblemen (A Once Upon a Rogue Regency Novels, Books 1-3)

Paranormal Books:

The Siren Saga

Echoes in the Silence, Book 1

About the Author

As a little girl I loved to create fantasy worlds and then give all my friends roles to play. Of course, I was always the heroine! Books have always been an escape for me and brought me so much pleasure, but it didn't occur to me that I could possibly be a writer for a living until I was in a career that was not my passion. One day, I decided I wanted to craft stories like the ones I loved, and with a great leap of faith I quit my day job and decided to try to make my dream come true. I discovered my passion, and I have never looked back. I feel incredibly blessed and fortunate that I have been able to make a career out of sharing the stories that are in my head! I write Scottish Medieval Romance, Regency Romance, and I have even written a Paranormal Romance book. And because I have the best readers in the world, I have hit the USA Today bestseller list several times.

If you love me, I hope you do!, you can follow me on Bookbub, and they will send you notices whenever I have a sale or a new release. You can follow me here:
bookbub.com/authors/julie-johnstone

You can also join my newsletter to get great prizes and inside scoops!

Join here:
www.juliejohnstoneauthor.com

I really want to hear from you! It makes my day!
Email me here:
juliejohnstoneauthor@gmail.com

I'm on Facebook a great deal chatting about books and life.
If you want to follow me, you can do so here:
facebook.com/authorjuliejohnstone

Can't get enough of me? Well, good! Come see me here:
Twitter:
@juliejohnstone
Goodreads:
https://goo.gl/T57MTA

Julie Recommends

The Pirate's Duchess: A SWASHBUCKLING Regency Historical Romance (A Regent's Revenge Novella Book 1) by Katherine Bone

Prologue

Letter from Lewis Barrett, Marquess of Eggleston, to His Grace, Richard Denzell, fifth Duke of Blackmoor, 23 September 1806

My Lord Duke,

It is with great sorrow that I must inform you we have been betrayed. Lord Underwood has undermined our adventures in copper and tin at Whitechurch, Eylesbarrow, and Mary Tavy. Desperate to recover our losses from those mines, I conferred with several bankers, who agreed selling our shares was in our best interest. To my shame, Lord Underwood bought them shortly afterward and profited £300,000. As a result, my family is penniless and my son will be shunned. Can such a thing be written with decided calm? I cannot bear the shame. There is only one escape: meeting my maker, knowing that you, of all capable men, whose authority and power surpass all but the king's, will ensure our heirs do not fall prey to a likewise scheme.

I beg you, keep our association secret. Do not reveal this letter or the source of the copper ore that Thomas

Davis discovered at your estate. If that information was to fall into the wrong hands, I believe Underwood would do anything to claim it, including commit murder.

Allow me, my faithful friend, to close my eyes one last time knowing that you will administer justice and ensure that my son, Algernon, does not suffer my fate. I go to my grave knowing he is in your capable hands.

I remain obedient,
Eggleston

One

SMUGGLING! If ever there was a need to TERMINATE this ill-timed enterprise, Trewman's Exeter Flying Post *insists the BLACK REGENT and his intolerable crew occasion the greatest enthusiasm and the hopes of mortals! Let it be known, ANYONE caught AIDING the cunning villain will be held LIABLE for damages and sent to ROUGEMONT.*

~ Trewman's Exeter Flying Post, *1 February 1807*

Exeter, Devon
April 1809

"Do you have everything you need, Your Grace?"

Prudence, the Duchess of Blackmoor nodded to Reverend Polidor Leyes, the vicar assigned to her soon-to-be father-in-law's estate, then clasped her dearest friend's hands as the chapel bells chimed ten times.

"Well," she said, smiling when the door closed, leaving the two of them alone again. "Today begins a new chapter of my life."

Lady Chloe Walsingham squeezed Prudence's hands and swung her arms wide to inspect her apple-green wedding gown. "You're a beautiful bride, Pru. And you deserve a happy ending."

Closing her eyes, Prudence glanced down at the intricate detail of her fruitful-colored gown, the yards of matching gossamer and lace, savoring the moment, and allowing herself to be transported back to the morning she'd married the man who owned her heart and soul—Tobias, the Duke of Blackmoor. Her breast had been full of boundless joy and love that momentous day. Strangely now, the bittersweet contrast between the virginal white she'd worn then and the gown she wore now, Tobias and her intended—Basil, Earl of Markwick—flashed in her mind's eye, teasing her with images of what could have been, of how deeply she could have loved, had a brutal fire not stolen her former husband's life.

Heat rose to her face as, once more, the stable's deadly flames hissed and crackled untamed before her like a hungry, writhing, poisonous viper sinking its fangs deep into her heart. Horses neighed. Men shouted.

Prudence grabbed her constricting throat.

"What is it?" Chloe asked, touching Prudence's cheek. "Are you overcome with emotion?"

The memories immediately silenced.

"You feel overly warm," her friend went on. "Perhaps you should sit down until the reverend returns."

Prudence inhaled a fortifying breath. "No," she said, forcing a smile. "On the contrary, I am quite well." She removed Chloe's hand and straightened her spine, determined more than ever to move on with her life.

It had been two years since fate had seared her heart to embers and labeled her a widow. She'd survived the devastating loss and the tempering that followed, allowing herself to be forged for a moment such as this. Why, then, when she had to speak her vows, did *that* fateful night play over and over again in her mind?

She walked past a table and a pair of chairs to the pitcher and bowl that were situated on a sideboard. She reached in, then dabbed cool water on her heated skin.

"Why are you so nervous? We've known the earl for years."

Prudence turned to find Chloe running her fingers along Mr. Leyes's excellent collection of literature assembled on the floor-to-ceiling shelves. She tried to push her concerns aside. "I shall endeavor to make him happy with all my heart."

Truth be told, she loved Basil. Did it matter that she wasn't *in* love with him?

For her, marriage had lost its romantic appeal the day she'd buried Tobias. These days, she didn't desire to be swept off her feet. What she needed now was companionship, a comfortable life, children.

Resigned to give Basil everything she had and more, she walked toward Chloe and led her away from the books. "Wish me luck?"

"Luck?" Chloe giggled the way she always did when she was about to make comparisons between them. "You are set to marry one of the most handsome, eligible men in all of Exeter. If anyone is in need of good fortune, it is I, Pru."

Prudence tsked. "That isn't true and you know it. You have much to offer any gentleman. Perhaps one sits in the rectory now, a handsome cavalier destined to whisk you away before the Season comes to an end."

"Not if my brother continues to scare them off." Chloe's brow furrowed like a petulant child's. "Oh, why did Pierce have to become a revenue officer?"

"Captain Walsingham is only doing his part."

"Yes. To ruin my life."

"Nay. To stand up to the Black Regent. Smugglers cannot be allowed to raid ships and sail the English Channel as if they are above the law. Think of the investors and merchants being put out of business." Basil's father, William, the Marquess of Underwood included. If Basil was correct, the marquess was on the brink of insolvency, which made his insistence on her marrying Basil understandable. Not only did Basil and Prudence care for each other dearly, but the unentailed lands Tobias had left her were worth at least ten thousand pounds a year.

"No," she said, determined to overcome any adversity. The Blackmoor estate would become her groom's, after all. "I heartily approve of the captain's pursuits. Your brother has done more for Exeter than anyone I know, and I'm glad of it."

Chloe crossed her arms over her elegant ecru gown. "No one can get past the drawbridge Pierce has levered at our door. No one."

"Drawbridge?" Prudence giggled. "Your brother isn't a villain from one of your Gothic novels, Chloe. He strives to protect you as diligently as he does our shipping lanes. The right man will come along. I urge you to be patient."

"Regretfully," Chloe said on a sigh, "patience isn't one of my strongest qualities."

It was true. Chloe was extremely impatient, and her impetuous actions kept the captain on his toes. "You have a caring nature, a highly prized quality in any woman and one not easily found these days. And I cherish you all the more for it."

"Oh, I do care, Pru. I really do. I want you to be happy." Chloe stepped back, clapped her hands over her mouth and then spread her arms. "I've always envied you. In my eyes, you *are* the luckiest woman in the world."

"I am"—she'd once considered herself lucky—"as light as a feather."

A feather disturbed by a sudden breeze.

"Who wouldn't be? You're about to marry the man you love. Is there anything more divine than that?"

Prudence gazed out the window of the stone chapel at the meadow that disappeared across the plateau leading to Blackmoor's property line. The acreage abutted Lord Underwood's estate and heralded prized orchards, hedgerows, fenced meadows, quarries, shapely knolls, and watercourses that fed the river below. But the manor house with its multiple stories of granite ashlar and wood withheld secrets she had yet to ascertain, information that had gone with Tobias to the grave, leaving her with no explanation why a map detailing another source of income on the estate had been locked away in his study.

"You aren't having second thoughts, are you?" Chloe crossed the distance and fingered Prudence's curls into place. "You have nothing to fear. Your father is in the chapel. And I saw your groom and Lord Underwood arrive nearly an hour ago."

Prudence sighed wistfully. "I know." She turned her thoughts to the aged marquess, imagining him standing in the church, hunched over his cane, measuring each person's worth and finding them lacking. A pincher who hoarded every farthing, Basil's father was a renowned curmudgeon.

"What then? Are you worried Lord Underwood and your father will come to blows?"

"No," she lied. Lord Underwood's gruff exterior and business tactics were legendary, and though her father approved of Basil, he was decidedly unapologetic in his opinions about Lord Underwood. He wasn't alone in those opinions, either.

She touched her lips, calmed by the memory of her intended's kiss. She'd endure Lord Underwood's intrusive opinions if it meant she gained the love and companionship of his son.

Prudence released a sigh and finally spoke to the heart of her worry. "Do you think I deserve a second chance at happiness, Chloe?"

Chloe's laughter caught her completely off guard. "Do frogs have warts?"

Prudence withheld her mirth. "Don't you mean toads?"

Chloe made a face. "Don't quibble. How many frogs did we kiss hoping one of them would turn into a prince?"

"One slimy creature was enough." At least neither of them had grown warts during their childhood experiment.

An enviable dimple appeared on Chloe's left cheek. Her unusual, but extraordinary violet eyes rounded, glistening with myriad emotions as she reached into her reticule and produced her copy of *The Castle of Otranto*.

"On page twenty-seven—"

"Please tell me you didn't bring *that* book to my wedding."

"I did," Chloe confirmed with a grin. "You know I never go anywhere without it. And I shall continue to read about blackguards and rogues while Markwick pampers you anon. I've never seen a man so smitten." She closed the book and hugged the volume close to her chest. She sighed distractedly. "How I long for a gentleman like the Earl of Markwick to do the same for me."

"That day will come," Prudence promised. "And when it does, your wallflower days will be all but forgotten."

Chloe released a hopeful sigh. "Do you think I shall find a man as worthy as Isabella's Theodore?"

"I know so." It was only fair. Chloe deserved a man who'd move heaven and earth to convey his love—a heroic man like Tobias.

I am such a fool hanging on to my ghosts. Tobias is gone. Basil is my future now.

"What I wouldn't give to meet a man as dashing as the Black Regent, though," Chloe said, drawing in another idealistic sigh.

Prudence released a horrified gasp. "The Black Regent? Why on earth would you glorify that rogue, especially when your brother is trying to catch him?"

"Bookkeepers under my brother's employ verified that local men are receiving stipends in their accounts when none were to be had. Does that not remind you of Robin Hood?" She stepped toward the mirror as if conveying mere gossip, rearranged an errant curl, then turned back to Prudence to put on her gloves. "I've overheard Pierce say the Regent's demeanor is darker than the clothes he wears. His ship, the *Fury*, is the wraith of the Cornish coast, painted blacker than night, and nigh uncatchable. You do know what this means, don't you?"

"No."

"He's even more complex than characters in our favorite tomes! How romantic!"

"A pirate? Preposterous!" How many times did she have to remind Chloe that the novels she read were works of fiction? "There is nothing romantic about pirates." Prudence eyed the door, counting down the moments until she was summoned, unsure she wanted to hear more shocking details. But for some inexplicable reason, she went on. "Tell me. What has *he* done now?"

Chloe's expression turned sheepish. "He targeted another one of Lord Underwood's ships."

"*Another* one?" she asked, lowering her voice to a whisper. If she knew one thing about Lord Underwood, it was this: he valued monetary worth over blood. And right now, with the dire straits he was already in financially, worry sunk deep in Prudence's belly.

"Yes, the cunning devil," Chloe continued. "He divided up the cargo and gave it to anyone who could carry it off the beach."

Prudence chewed the inside of her lower lip. "Why wasn't I informed about this earlier?"

"I assume Markwick didn't want to worry you about it before the wedding."

Prudence toyed with the Honiton lace at her wrists as her friend went on. "I'm sure the earl waits to divulge this unhappy state of affairs after your wedding night. Men do not feel obliged to burden women with their concerns."

Pru looked up at Chloe sharply. "I am not most women."

"Oh yes. I am well aware of that, dear friend. I feel positive Markwick simply wants to preserve your happiness, rather than encumber you with his father's difficulties."

Prudence tapped her bottom lip, then sighed. "I suppose you are right. Go on. Tell me what else you've heard."

Chloe's eyes brightened. "After the pirate's last attack," she said, thankfully leaving out her usual litany of the devil's misdeeds, "The Captain was forced to escort debt collectors from Lord Underwood's offices."

"You *can* use your brother's name when we're alone, Chloe."

Her brows furrowed. She gulped. "Forgive me. Old habits. You know how demanding he is."

"I do." Prudence had also known Underwood was struggling, but was the marquess *destitute*?

"I assure you, these are not yarns. Not in the least. Pierce has it on good authority—"

"Your brother has been feeding your imagination

again."

Chloe's smile faltered. "Balderdash."

Prudence fanned herself more rapidly. "I'm surprised that you, of all people, believe your brother's stories. Even if he does work with the Royal Navy and the Revenue Office, don't you remember how he deceived both of us into believing we could swim?"

"But now we *can* swim," Chloe said, leaving out the horrific way they'd learned to do so. "I've been telling you for nigh a year now that Pierce has chased the *Fury* out of the quay, down the Exe River, and into the Lyme Sea and never once caught it. He calls it a ghost ship manned by demons."

Prudence shivered. She wasn't comfortable talking about ghosts.

"The Black Regent," Chloe said breathlessly, eyes wide, "is as real as you and me, and thankfully so."

"How naive you are. The brigand is an elaborate sham conjured by free traders to cover up their own tracks. Or worse, he's been invented by your brother to veil his inability to catch the marauder preying upon my future father-in-law's assets."

"Do you really think my brother would be so cruel?"

Prudence arched her brow and cast Chloe a meaningful glare.

Chloe picked up her reticule with a soft huff, shoved her book inside it, and hugged the bag tightly to her just as the door to the room creaked on its hinges. She stepped forward expectantly as the gray-haired clergyman reappeared.

"Apologies for the delay, Your Grace," he said. "We are ready for you."

The old wooden door creaked more as it moved farther

outward on its hinges, casting shadows on the wall beside it. Her father, Cyril, Marquess of Heathcote appeared. "The time has come, daughter. Are you ready?"

"Yes." She nodded, determined to put the Black Regent and Lord Underwood's financial difficulties out of her mind.

She and Chloe exchanged an emotional embrace, despite their quarrel. "Do not worry. It will be wonderful, Pru."

"Indeed," her father added. He took hold of Prudence's hand and placed it in the crook of his arm, glancing down at her with genuine affection. "We mustn't keep your young gentleman waiting any longer."

"No." The thrumming wings in her stomach dissipated at the thought of Basil. She'd been through hell and looked forward to spending the rest of her life with a loving friend.

He patted her hand. She leaned her head against his shoulder and squeezed his arm.

They followed Chloe toward the rectory, and as the chapel doors opened, Chloe flashed them one more smile before she disappeared through them.

Prudence stood at the threshold with her father, looking out into the chapel. The pews were radiantly lined with flowers in shades of white and green, all leading up to where Basil patiently waited. His handsome face was eclipsed, his thick dark hair illuminated by fragments of light shining through the stained glass.

Father patted her hand again and gazed down at her fondly. "Shall we do this, my dear?"

She nodded. "Yes. I am ready."

Her father wasted no time guiding her to the altar, past faces she'd known long and well, servants devoted to her as a child and, since her husband's death, Blackmoor's tenants, as well as notable gentry.

"It's been two years since the duke's passing," someone whispered to her left.

Prudence pressed forward, past rightful members of the *ton* seated near the front.

"Imagine being a widow at three and twenty," another voice said softly.

Tobias's face momentarily replaced Basil's, and her slipper caught on the hem of her gown. Father's quick reflexes kept her from falling flat on her face before Basil, God, and their guests.

He squeezed her arm reassuringly. "Do not listen to foolish hen prattle, my dear. The earl is waiting for you."

Straightening her shoulders, she focused on Basil's handsome face and light-blue eyes that glinted like Blackmoor silver, twinkling, promising years of fidelity and conveying assurances that all would be well. Tall, lean, and clothed in simple black and white, Basil gave her a pleasant smile that lured her to him, and warmth swept through her. *He* was her future now. No more sleepless nights lying awake, feeling helpless and alone. No more nightmares or thoughts of what could have been.

Her father stopped just before the altar and placed a kiss on her brow. "Your mother would be so proud of you if she were here. You are strong, my girl."

"Thank you, Papa," she whispered, her heart filled with gratitude.

He turned her toward Basil, who sketched a bow, then lowered his hand and helped her step up to the altar. When she finally stood beside him, he raised her hand to his lips, kissing the amethyst ring on her right hand before clicking his heels together with practiced ease.

He leaned down to whisper in her ear as he removed her veil. "No regrets?"

"None."

"I promise you'll never have them."

"I accept your challenge," she replied, returning Basil's smile.

Together, they turned to Mr. Leyes, who stood like a rotund badger in front of his den, a book held open in each hand. He nodded to Prudence and Basil, then began reading from the first book, a copy of *Fordyce's Sermons*.

Throughout Leyes's literal depiction of a woman's character, Basil held her hand in his, gently rubbing her knuckles with his thumb as brilliant light filtered through the windows behind the vicar's back, bathing them in prisms of color.

Leyes paused, then said, "Is anyone present who can justifiably object to the joining of this man and woman in holy wedlock?"

Someone cleared his throat, and Prudence's breath hitched. When the vicar craned his head to find the instigator, the room fell silent. Then Leyes nodded, smiling confidently at Basil, who turned to take hold of both her hands and gazed into her eyes.

"Basil Halford, Earl of Markwick, do you take Prudence Denzell, Duchess of Blackmoor, to wed?"

The doors to the chapel slammed open.

"I d—"

"He does *not*," came a deep, angry voice from the back.

That voice! It can't be . . .

Prudence's body tensed. Surely she'd heard wrong.

She turned away from the vicar and Basil to see a cloaked man standing in dark silhouette, holding a silver cane. There was something ill-omened about the way he stood and angled his head. Her heart clenched, then raced.

"What is the meaning of this?" Basil asked, anger rolling off him in waves. "How dare you interrupt our wedding?"

"*No one* is going to marry *my* wife today."

Made in the USA
Columbia, SC
11 March 2023

13629172R00109